Nine Lives to Murder

MARIAN BABSON

Nine Lives to Murder

St. Martin's Press
New York

Library of Congress Cataloging-in-Publication Data

Babson, Marian.
Nine lives to murder / Marian Babson.
p.   cm.
"A Thomas Dunne book."
ISBN 0-312-10511-8 (hardcover)
1. Actors—England—Fiction.   2. Metamorphosis—
Fiction.   3. Cats—Fiction.   I. Title.
PS3552.A25N56   1994
813'.54—dc20   93-45286   CIP

First published in Great Britain by HarperCollins Publishers.

First U.S. Edition: April 1994
10 9 8 7 6 5 4 3 2 1

To
All the cats in our lives—
and the life in our cats

He lay still. Absolutely still. The cold hard surface beneath him was becoming colder and harder by the moment, but he could not bear the thought of moving, of getting up and seeking the deep luxurious comfort of his own bed.

It seemed to him that he had tried moving at some point in the recent past and the pain had been so excruciating that he had abandoned the idea, perhaps for ever. Rather than face pain like that again, he would lie here like a marble statue for the rest of time. At the very least, he would lie doggo until he was able to pinpoint the source of the pain and remember where it had come from . . . and why.

Lie doggo . . . ugh! What a revolting concept. What a disgusting word. He made a little noise deep in his throat; it sounded almost like a growl.

Had he had a heart attack? That was always a prime consideration in a man of his age and, well, size. He had given up cigarettes, after a mortal struggle, some years ago. But it had not been so easy to forgo the steaks, the clotted cream, the claret and burgundy and all those delicious little nibbles at all those Opening Night—yes, and Closing Night—parties.

This time, his stomach growled.

But his heart remained steady. It was beating slowly but sturdily, no hint of pain radiating from it. No, something deep within himself told him that a heart attack could be ruled out.

What else, then? Wait . . . wait . . . something was flickering at the back of his mind, trying to get through to him. A faint auditory memory of noise: voices, shouts, wood clattering, an almighty crash, a woman screaming.

An accident. That must have been it. He was conscious

of a feeling of relief. Not, then, the betrayal from within of a weakened artery or failing organ, but an accident. An accident was understandable. Acceptable.

Was it? What kind of accident? A car crash? He had always warned Miranda that she drove too fast, but she was moderately careful. Geoffrey, on the other hand, drove like an accident looking for a place to happen. Surely he hadn't been fool enough to step into any vehicle that had his son at the wheel?

Where was Miranda? Why wasn't she here? He caught himself just as he was about to stir restlessly. No, mustn't move. Wasn't safe to move. Not yet. But where was everybody? Where was Miranda? Where, even, was Geoffrey?

Had they all abandoned him? Crashed and run? Leaving him here, perhaps thrown clear of the wreckage and out of sight in some gully while rescuers conveyed the others, unconscious, to the nearest hospital? Had the rescuers overlooked him?

Or was he the sole survivor? Thrown clear while the others perished in a fiery holocaust? What others? Who had been with him? Where had they been going?

Muddy thinking. He wasn't outdoors; he could feel a building sheltering him; smell the familiar smells of the theatre.

Probably a slight concussion. He could hope it was slight. His head ached abominably, but he didn't feel strong enough to get up and search for some aspirins. Moving might make it worse. Better to lie absolutely still and try to remember what had happened.

Miranda had figured prominently in it. He could vaguely remember her screaming. 'Alley cat! You have the morals of an alley cat!'

Oh dear, she'd found out about Cynthia. Or possibly Jilly. Impossible to keep a secret for long around here. Theatre people gossiped too much.

She'd been throwing things, too. Had she hit him? Unlikely. Her aim wasn't that good. And his agility was legendary. Ten years of living with Miranda had given him a set of reflexes that were the envy of young men half his age. All their jogging and gym workouts couldn't produce the flexibility gained by having to sidestep the blows and missiles of an irate woman.

But something had hit him. A throb—more of a recollection than a current pain—somewhere in the middle of his spine told him that. Then there had been a strong sensation of falling . . . the crash . . . the pain . . . the screaming . . .

How long ago? Hours rather than minutes. Hours? . . . It couldn't be. They wouldn't have left him lying on the cold floor all that time.

Unless he was mortally injured. Couldn't be moved. Broken back, perhaps? Too dangerous to move him. Specialists flying in from all over the world to assess the situation and give their opinions.

He was Winstanley Fortescue, leading Shakespearean actor, but also brilliant comedian in modern farces, as well as a sensitive and thoughtful interpreter of the latest drama, whether commercial or avant-garde . . .

Husband of the glamorous post-ingénue, Miranda Everton, for the past eight years; father (by a very early and ill-fated marriage) of the brilliant young juvenile, Geoffrey Fortescue (treading, perhaps a trifle too closely, on his father's heels, but that could be dealt with in due course. Young Pup!)

Winstanley Fortescue, not to put too fine a point on it, was a Titan of the English Stage. Oh yes, they'd come running from all over the world to put *him* together again after his fall.

But where were they? Why was he lying here alone?

And where was 'here'? He risked a quick split-second raising of his eyelids. On the floor, just as he had suspected.

It wasn't right. There was something wrong about it; deeply wrong; disturbingly wrong. His eyes had closed again automatically and he shrank from trying to force them open again.

If only he could *think*. Think properly, his mind un-clouded by the thundering headache.

Headache . . . he tested the idea. No, not the same as a hangover. He hadn't tied one on and crept under a table to sleep it off since the early days in Rep—and not very often then. He placed too much value on The Instrument to risk ruining his health. No, no, there had been an accident, a terrible freak accident.

Even so, he couldn't lie here all day . . . or was it all night? He was feeling better . . . slightly better. The pain seemed to have localized now; it was all compressed into that harsh throbbing headache. He might just risk moving. Slowly and carefully.

He began with his fingers, flexing them cautiously. They seemed to be in working order, but felt vaguely awkward, as though he had something caught between each one. Of course! For an instant the image flickered through his mind of his fingers clawing at the curtains as he fell, trying to break his fall. Shreds of the material must still be twisted round them.

Feeling slightly comforted, he extended his arms, then relaxed them again. Yes, everything all right there. With more anxiety, he stretched one leg, then the other. So far, so good.

He rested then, trying to come to terms with his greatest terror before testing it. Although you could move your arms and legs, your back could still be broken.

Now . . . courage to the sticking point . . . *try*.

His head rolled backward . . . good, neck all right. His back arched smoothly and without undue pain. Nothing wrong there. The tip of his tail twitched.

The . . . *tip*? Of his . . . *tail*? . . . *Twitched*?

His eyes flew open. He raised his hands in front of them. One soft furry white paw and one soft furry black paw seemed to swim in the air before him. He flexed his fingers and claws sprang out from between the small delicate pads.

'*Miranda!*' he roared. '*Miranda!*'

It came out: '*Mirreeow!*'

2

'What was that?' Entering the star dressing-room she shared with her husband, Miranda Everton Fortescue paused and looked around.

'What was what?' Davy Bentham asked.

Immediately behind her, the small protective group huddled closer, as though they could shield her from the nightmare that had already happened.

'I didn't hear—' Tottie Clayton broke off as the noise came again.

'*Mirreeow!*' They'd heard it often enough before, why should it send a cold chill down their spines now?

'Monty!' Tottie cried. 'It's poor old Monty!'

'Monty! Where is he?' Miranda started towards the sound, towards the stage.

'Never mind the cat.' Davy tried to steer her into the dressing-room. 'He's all right. You need some rest.'

'No!' Miranda struggled to break free of his grasp. 'He might be badly injured. You saw what happened. He might—'

'I'll get him,' Tottie said quickly. 'You go with Davy. I'll bring him in to you.'

'That's right.' Davy succeeded in moving her into the dressing-room and eased her down on to the chaise-longue. 'You just worry about yourself for a bit. You've had a nasty shock. Let me get you a drink.'

'We could all use a drink,' Cynthia Vernon said querulously. 'Miranda isn't the only one who got a shock. What do we do about the show now?'

'It's not up to me. There's a big advance sale, but without Win . . .' Davy shrugged. 'We might be able to postpone the opening for a while if . . .' He stopped unhappily, letting them all finish the sentence for themselves.

If it looks as though Win might pull through . . .
If Win is able to work again . . .
If Win makes it . . .

'See to the drinks, Davy, please.' Miranda's voice betrayed her struggle to keep from breaking down. 'If Win has left anything in the hospitality cabinet.'

'Right away!' He got her drink first, then ranged the bottles on top of the cabinet, leaving the others to help themselves.

'God, what a mess!' Geoffrey poured a large Scotch with a shaking hand. 'Do you think I should let Mother know? And Jennet?'

'It would be kinder than letting them find out through the media.' Miranda sipped at her drink with an air of conscious restraint. 'I'll ring Antoinette myself, if you like.'

'Thanks, that might be best.' Their eyes met in tacit recognition of the difficult situation.

'Here he is!' Tottie entered, carrying a large black and white cat. 'Still a bit groggy, poor old boy. But there doesn't seem to be any lasting damage.'

'You can't be sure,' Miranda said. 'That was a terrible knock he took. It might be better to have the vet check him out.'

The cat growled.

'Be careful,' Tottie warned. 'He understands more than you think. Don't you, old boy?' She cuddled him, nuzzling her head against his.

'Oh, forget the tatty old thing!' Cynthia snapped. 'We have *serious* problems here. We can't waste time worrying about a cat.'

The cat narrowed his eyes and stared at her thoughtfully.

'You wouldn't say that if it were your cat,' Tottie said.

'The Duchess of Malfi is a pedigree Persian.' Cynthia was at her frostiest. 'There's no comparison.'

'I'll take responsibility for Monty,' Davy said resignedly. 'He's the theatre cat and I'm the Stage Manager—he *must* come under my department—everything else does. Just let him rest a bit and, if he doesn't perk up within a reasonable time, I'll take him to the—' he hesitated and glanced at Monty—'the v-e-t.'

The cat twitched his whiskers. It gave him the appearance of sneering.

'I think he's learned to spell,' Tottie said. 'At least, certain words.'

'Will you forget the damned cat!' Cynthia snarled. 'What are we going to do about the show?'

'The thing is, dear,' Tottie said, 'it's easier to worry about the cat than the show. That's out of our hands right now.'

The telephone burred sharply, startling them all. Miranda started for it, then faltered. 'It might be the hospital—'

'I'll take it.' Davy snatched up the telephone, but hesitated and sent an imploring glance heavenwards before he spoke.

'Good evening. Chesterton Theatre . . . Oh, hello, Jilly.'

Miranda made a brief dismissive gesture and returned to the chaise-longue.

'Sorry, Jilly.' Davy took up his cue. 'Afraid Win isn't available right now. No, nor Miranda either. You'll have to make do with me.'

Cynthia poured herself another drink, the top of the bottle rattling angrily against the rim of the glass.

'Really? Where did you hear that, Jilly?' Davy covered the mouthpiece with one hand and turned to Miranda. 'Do we want to make any statement to the Press?'

'Not yet.' Miranda leaned back and closed her eyes. 'And never to *her*.'

The cat mewled plaintively and began struggling to escape Tottie's arms.

'Look, Jilly, it's all a bit chaotic here at the moment. I can't really talk now . . . What? Who told you that? . . . No, no, I can't confirm anything—I didn't say I denied it . . . not exactly—' Davy squirmed uncomfortably as the

voice at the other end of the line chattered at him remorse-
lessly.

'Look, Jilly, I'm only the Stage Manager. Let me get
someone with more authority to ring you back . . . I
promise . . . as soon as possible. What? . . . Well, yes, there
was a bit of an accident, but it's too early to . . . I can't
really—' He pulled the telephone away from his ear and
looked at it incredulously.

'She hung up on me,' he told the others.

'Well, that fat's in the fire now,' Tottie said fatalistically.

'A *bit* of an accident!' Cynthia laughed harshly. 'Win's
on a life-support machine in the Intensive Care Unit, for
God's sake!'

There was a thud as the cat hit the ground. He staggered
across the floor, legs not quite coordinating, and sprang
into Miranda's lap. He lurched up face to face with her, his
claws digging into the soft fabric of her blouse as he clutched
at her.

'*Mirreeow* . . .' he wailed. '*Mirreeow!*'

3

It was dark when he opened his eyes again. Dark inside the
large familiar room and dark outside. It took him a few
moments to become aware of this. He could see perfectly
well, if a bit simplistically.

A bit . . . A long shudder rippled through him. The events
of the past few hours began returning. It wasn't true. It
couldn't be true. He'd been having a nightmare.

That's right. A nightmare. There was Miranda's dear
face on the pillow beside him. He'd wake her and they'd
have a good laugh about it.

He stretched out his arm to shake her, then stared unbelievingly at the long furry extension that had moved in
answer to his brain's command. He let his head fall back

on the pillow with a low moan. He was awake—and he was still trapped in the nightmare.

Or was this some sort of punishment for the life he had led? Had he died and been reincarnated as the alley cat Miranda had accused him of being in their last quarrel?

But—he felt a flash of indignation—surely when one was reincarnated, one returned at the birth of the new being. Why should he have made his return in an already existing body? A second-hand body. And a cat's body at that.

It might have been worse, some corner of his mind suggested. He might have come back as a cockroach. He had always been revolted by Kafka. He'd even scorned *archy and mehitabel*.

So why had he wound up as *mehitabel*? Or, rather, as Montmorency, the theatre cat? Mind you, he'd always had a soft spot for old Monty, but this was carrying it too far. What had gone wrong? If some Day of Judgement had come and sentence had been passed upon him, why couldn't he remember it?

But wait . . . he wasn't dead yet. He knew that because he had heard them all talking. He was still alive. He was hitched up to a life-support machine in an Intensive Care Unit.

Or . . . Monty was.

4

The cat woke Miranda with his restlessness. She stirred and whimpered softly, trying to hold on to sleep, some instinct warning her that consciousness would be too unpleasant to face. She had almost succeeded in sinking back into deep slumber when the cat yowled, as though in agony. It brought her sitting upright, heart racing.

The cat was sitting up, too, looking around with dazed bewilderment. Definitely, she must get the vet in to see to him first thing in the morning. The poor creature was probably concussed out of his tiny mind.

Realizing that she was awake, the cat moved closer, rubbing against her, uttering small sounds of distress.

'Poor old boy.' She cuddled him absently. 'You miss Win, don't you? So do I, bastard that he was—*is*. Don't worry—' she was speaking to herself more than to the cat now. 'We'll get him back.'

The agonizing noises came again. Miranda reached out and snapped on the bedside lamp. The poor creature must be in genuine pain. She wondered whether she dared disturb the vet at this hour. Then she realized that she didn't know the vet's number. She would have to disturb Davy first to get it. And poor Davy needed his sleep; he, too, had had a rough day.

'*Mirreeow*,' the cat wailed, trying to burrow into her side. '*Mirreeow*.'

'Poor old Monty, you never knew what hit you, did you?' She stroked him, her fingers probing gently for evidence of broken bones. He was moving more easily than he had been earlier and nothing seemed too obviously wrong. She had heard that cats had great recuperative powers, but could she depend on that?

Monty was in great distress and making her feel guiltier by the minute. They should have called the vet for him immediately, but there had been all the horror of Win lying unconscious on the floor and the rush to get an ambulance and follow it to the hospital. Poor Monty had been lost and forgotten in the shuffle. Then, when they had found him again upon returning to the theatre, they had been in the later stages of shock, with the contingent exhaustion and lassitude that made even the simplest decisions seem too hard to cope with. It had been easier to bring him home with her, which was what he had seemed to want, and worry about everything else in the morning.

But not this early in the morning. She glanced at the tiny enamelled clock on the bedside table. Four a.m., traditionally the hour of least resistance, when the tides of life ebbed to their lowest and the dying slipped away.

Win! She snatched up the telephone and stabbed blindly at the buttons, the number already committed to memory. They wouldn't be sleeping there.

It took too many rings before anyone answered. Long enough for panic to begin fluttering her heart. Surely they shouldn't be too busy to answer the phone—not at this hour. Unless they were dealing with an emergency. *Win—?*

Then a low pleasant voice spoke in her ear, a voice trained to inspire immediate confidence. There was never any emergency at St Monica's; Win was in the best of hands; everything possible was being done for him.

'Good morning, this is Miranda Fortescue. I'm sorry to disturb you at this hour, but I wanted to inquire about my husband . . .'

'Oh yes, Mrs Fortescue. His condition is stable . . .'

That meant no change, didn't it? Win was still lying there like a log—or a fallen giant. Unconscious and helpless, fighting for his life. Kept alive by a machine . . .

The comfortable banal phrases flowed through the earpiece to her, but the voice wasn't inspiring so much confidence now.

'Monty, stop it!' She struggled briefly with the cat, who was rubbing against her face, trying to insinuate his head between her own head and the telephone, as though he was trying to hear what was being said at the other end. Jealous, probably, because her attention was no longer centred on him.

'I see, thank you.' She brushed the cat aside and ended the conversation. One-sided as it was, it wasn't going anywhere. Hospitals never wanted to tell you anything. Only that the patient was stable . . . resting comfortably . . . still alive. That was what she had called to find out.

'Goodbye.' She replaced the phone in its cradle and

suddenly swept Monty into her arms, burying her face in his fur. After a brief, surprised wriggle, he lay quietly in her arms while her tears drenched his neck.

5

He closed his eyes, feeling the melancholy wash over him like the tears. Miranda, Miranda, you *do* love me. And I love you. And what's to come of us now?

She began stroking him softly, hypnotically, in rhythm with her sobs. He relaxed into her caress until, suddenly, she touched the wrong spot on his head and pain flared through him. He wrenched away, hissing a protest, and leaped to the floor.

'Oh, poor Monty,' she apologized. 'I forgot your head must be sore. Did it hurt you dreadfully when Win collided with you? Come here and let me see if you've got a lump there. Come on, that's a good boy, I'll be careful. I won't hurt you any more. Let me just feel your head . . .'

Against his better judgement, he allowed himself to be coaxed back on to the bed. He moved slowly, cautiously, his head complaining all the way. Yes, it did hurt dreadfully —both now and when the accident had happened.

Gently, Miranda's fingers probed the delicate spot between his ears, but not quite gently enough. He flinched away, involuntarily spitting at her. With the pain came a sudden flash of recognition—and memory.

A disquieting double-image formed in his mind, as though he was remembering the accident from both points of view: the giant form hurtling towards the small furry body; the little head rearing back, ears flattened, eyes narrowed to terrified hostile points. The clattering of poles, slats and boards as the makeshift rehearsal set collapsed around them. Then the crash and the blinding pain on both sides as they collided head on.

Head on. Forehead to forehead. He had read somewhere that the essential elements of personality were contained in the frontal lobes of the brain. In the force of the encounter, had some sort of mad exchange taken place? It was some sort of explanation anyway. *There are more things in heaven and earth, Horatio . . .*

There was another remembered pain, though . . . one not quite simultaneous with the collision, but just slightly preceding it. A sharp, shooting pain in the small of his back. *His* back . . . or Monty's? He had seen one of the stage hands slam a broom handle across Monty's back once. After he had threatened the stage hand with dismissal, it had never happened again. Or was it just that he had never caught the man doing it again?

'Poor Monty,' Miranda crooned. 'It's a hard life.'

She had no idea how hard. He nudged her perfunctorily with his nose, already trying to project his problems into the future, trying to find some solution to them.

'Oh, Monty, Monty, Monty!' Miranda held him close as the tears overwhelmed her again. 'Oh, Win, Win, Win! What are we going to do?'

The knock at the door startled them both. Automatically, Miranda glanced at the clock again. Still just a few minutes past four. She'd only just spoken with St Monica's; there was no time for Win to have died and a policeman to be mobilized to come and break the news to her. They wouldn't do it that way, would they? Not when she had just been talking to them . . . ?

'Are you all right, dear?' The doorknob turned, the door swung open. 'It's me, Tottie. I heard your voice. Were you calling? I couldn't be sure.'

'Oh, Tottie!' Miranda had forgotten that their old friend and current wardrobe mistress had volunteered to stay the night—in case. In case of what was tactfully not specified and, while Miranda did not expect to break down even if the news were bad, she found that she was not averse to having a friendly presence nearby.

'I've just been talking to the hospital and,' Miranda admitted with a rueful smile, 'the cat.'

'Monty's good company.' Tottie came over and perched on the side of the bed, reaching out to stroke the cat. 'He's deserted his Tottie tonight. He knows you need him more.'

'There's no change.' Miranda answered the unspoken question.

'I didn't expect there would be. It's too early, isn't it?' The hand stroking Monty's fur tightened convulsively and he knew there was more wrong than Tottie was admitting. 'These things take a while.'

'I suppose so.' Miranda drew a deep unsteady breath. 'At least he's getting the best of care. I've been in St Monica's enough myself to know how good they are. Tomorrow we'll contact the best specialists available. We'll have Win back on his feet in no time. Back in the theatre.'

'That's right, dear.' A handful of flesh and fur was gripped and twisted. 'Everything will look better in the morning—the real morning, when there's daylight outside.'

The cat gave a small protesting mew and tried to writhe out of her grasp.

'We'll all feel better in the morning,' Tottie insisted, tightening her hold on the cat. 'Perhaps you need to take another sleeping pill, dear. Just one doesn't seem to be working.'

'I don't want a sleeping pill.' Miranda turned her head, avoiding Tottie's accusing gaze—thus telling her that she hadn't taken the first one. 'I'm all right. I'm not the one you have to worry about.'

'Too true, dear,' Tottie said in heartfelt tones. 'But we have to watch over you as well. The last thing in the world we need is for you to go on the sick list, too.'

'I won't,' Miranda promised. 'I've got to be strong now —for Win.' A brooding look came into her eyes. 'Whether he deserves it or not.'

'*Mirreeow!*' the cat protested.

'All right, Monty, all right. I know what you want.' Tottie stood and picked him up. 'You just come with me. He wants his litter-box, that's what he wants.'

6

His litter-box? Winstanley Fortescue, foremost Shakespearean actor of his generation, brilliant comedy player, prospective Knight of the Realm (there had been discreet soundings; if not this Honours List, then the next, or perhaps the next). Winstanley Fortescue, scooped up like a diapered babe and carried off to a litter-box!

'I'm afraid we don't have a litter-box,' Miranda said. 'We don't usually have a cat around.'

'Oh, that's all right, dear. He prefers his litter-box, but he can make do with a newspaper now and then. I'd put him out in the garden, but I'm afraid he might wander off and this is a strange neighbourhood to him.'

'Yes . . .' Miranda's thoughts were obviously already far away. She reached for a pad and pen on the bedside table. 'I suppose I'd better make a list of things that need to be done . . .'

'Don't work too long, dear. Put out the light soon and try to get some rest.'

'Yes . . .' Abstractedly, Miranda made a note.

At the door, Tottie hesitated. She opened her mouth, closed it again, opened it again. 'If you want anything, just call.' Her fingers twined nervously in Monty's fur. That wasn't what she had intended to say, but it would have to do.

'I'll be all right,' Miranda said. 'Get some rest yourself, Tottie.'

'Yes, I'll just get Monty settled first.' This time she stepped outside and closed the door. 'Oh, Monty!' She hugged the cat tighter, resting her forehead on his back. 'Monty, Monty, what are we going to do?'

Damn it! Didn't any of these women own handkerchiefs? He wrinkled his fur against the dampness soaking into it and voiced a protest.

'Yes, yes, we'll get you there.' She misunderstood the nature of his complaint. Or did she? He became aware of an increasing urgency, now that the matter had been called to mind.

Nevertheless, he was affronted when she dumped him down on the Sports Pages and stood back expectantly. He sat down deliberately and glared at her.

'Go on,' she said. 'You know what that's for. You just go ahead and use it now.' And stood there. Watching.

He glared at her, but she didn't seem to notice. An absent look had come into her eyes, as though her thoughts had slipped away to some far distant place . . . or problem.

'I don't know,' she said softly to herself. 'I just don't know.'

He settled himself firmly on the paper, prepared to out-wait her. For once in his life, he had no desire for an audience. In his irritation, his tail lashed back and forth. He tried to stop it, but the control mechanism escaped him; the tail seemed to have acquired a life of its own. After a brief struggle, he abandoned the attempt. Let it lash, it suited his mood.

The swishing sound on the paper brought Tottie back to attention. 'Oh, you're in *that* mood, are you?' She shrugged. 'Well, you can't have it your own way. I'm not letting you outside. Be a good boy and use the paper. You'll be back to the theatre and your litter-box tomorrow.'

It wasn't his intention to flatten his ears, but he felt them go down. Deliberately, he got up, turned his back on her, and sat down again, tail still lashing. Really, a cat's body was quite expressive. He had noticed this in a desultory sort of way before; now he began to appreciate the extent of it.

'Well, I'm sorry.' Tottie had no difficulty interpreting his fury. 'But that's the way it is. I can's stand around waiting for you to resign yourself, I've got things to do.' He heard her leave the room.

After a few moments he got up and turned around, checking. Yes, she was gone—and not lurking in the hall outside to make sure he used the paper. He could do so now in decent privacy. But first . . .

Awkwardly, but with increasing expertise, he used his claws (handy little gadgets) to rifle through the pages until he found the Theatre Section.

There! *There* it was . . . the bloated porcine face of Oliver Crump (better known in theatrical circles as Oliver Grump), the sadist who purported to be a drama critic. The monster who was actually *paid* for destroying the hopes, dreams and ambitions of talented people so far above him that, were there any justice in the world, he would not be allowed to breathe the same air, let alone sit in judgement of them.

Everyone knew the swine had started out as a restaurant critic—and that was where he should have stayed. With any luck, he could have then eaten his way into an early grave, whether through stuffing himself until he burst, or whether through ptomaine or botulism poisoning judiciously engendered by an enraged restaurateur. And don't think there hadn't been a few rumours about *that*. The whisper was that the increasing frequency of gastric attacks had been the reason for his transfer to the theatre assignment. With his bulk, he had not been able to maintain the anonymity required of a restaurant critic and there were more than a few *maître-d's* who would have considered a burst of short unfortunate publicity a small price to pay for the removal of such a snail in their salad.

Actors had no such redress. Not usually.

He positioned himself over the hated face and relieved decades of injured feelings, along with a couple of other things. It appeared that there was going to be a certain amount of compensation to being in this situation. *Heh-heh-heh* . . .

He had retreated to a far corner of the room and suc-
cumbed to an irresistible urge to wash his face when a
sudden stirring of curiosity halted his paw in mid-swipe.

Tottie had departed saying that she had things to see to.
At four-thirty in the morning? What things?

He became aware of voices . . . No, one voice, murmur-
ing softly . . . Telephoning someone? At this hour?

Purposefully, he padded down the hallway to the drawing-room.

Tottie sat curled in one corner of one of the velvet-
upholstered sofas flanking the fireplace. Her feet were
tucked under her but, although she looked comfortable, she
did not sound as though she felt comfortable.

'I tried.' She sounded apologetic. 'I tried to prepare her
for it, but my heart failed me. Two or three times I tried
to sort of suggest it, but I just couldn't do it. Let her have
at least one good night's sleep before she faces it.'

There was a prolonged burst of dialogue from the other
end of the line, to which Tottie listened, nodding her head
as though her agreement could be seen. 'I know, Rufus,'
she moaned. 'I know . . .'

What did she know? What did they all know that he
didn't? He leaped to the arm of the sofa and from there to
the back, trying to insinuate his head between Tottie's ear
and the phone.

'. . . pull the plug . . .' the voice was saying.

'I know it's sensible to think about it, but . . .' Tottie
began sniffling again. 'It's too soon. It's much too soon.
They can't be sure, not just like that. They must need more
time, more tests . . . oh, it's terrible. With all his faults, no
one would ever have wanted him to end up like that . . .'

Faults? What faults? He reared back and glared at her. She
was talking about *him*, he knew it. But what was going on?
He tried to deny the knowledge creeping into his consciousness. *Plug? Plug?* Was that just slang, or was it a literal
statement of fact? How badly had he been injured?

'I expect the rest of them will be here in the morning.'

Tottie was answering an unheard question. 'Burt is trying to contact Sir Reginald—wouldn't you just know he'd be visiting Los Angeles at a time like this? With the time difference, Burt will be up all night. Not that any of us can sleep right now . . .' She sniffled into incoherency.

The click at the other end of the line was decisive. Good old Rufus was not about to lose any more sleep himself.

'Oh, Monty, Monty . . .' Tottie replaced the receiver and swept the cat into her arms before he could get away. She buried her face in the back of his neck. 'What are we going to do?'

Good question. He didn't know what she was going to do, but it was becoming increasingly clear that he had to get himself over to St Monica's, sneak into the Intensive Care Unit—and take a good look at what was happening to his own body.

7

After a brief struggle to escape, he settled down with an appearance of docility to wait until Tottie's attention was elsewhere. Strangely, he found the gentle stroke of her hand soothing and soporific. His eyes began to close and an involuntary reaction began deep in his throat. He realized he was purring.

Fascinated, he began experimenting to control it. At first, this resulted in a series of hiccoughy interruptions in the smooth flow of sound.

'Monty, are you all right?' Tottie was alarmed. 'Got a hairball?' She began patting him on the back vigorously. 'Cough it up, there's a good boy.'

He gave her an indignant glare and took a deep breath. Left to its automatic mechanism, the purr resumed steadily.

'That's better.' Tottie seemed to find the purr as soothing as he found her stroking. 'Don't let anything happen to you, Monty. I couldn't bear it if I lost my little gentleman friend.'

Well! Who'd have thought Tottie had such a sentimental streak in her? She'd certainly never given any sign of it when she was berating artistes for the way they maltreated their costumes. Only last week she'd snapped at him and nearly struck him, simply because his lace cuff had caught on a loose nail and torn. A very small tear, the audience would never have seen it, but Tottie had gone berserk. And it had all been the fault of the careless stagehand who had neglected to knock in the nail properly. It had been a danger to the actors, sticking out like that; it could just as easily have been flesh that had torn. Not the first time Woody had been guilty of negligence, either, even his Union had been forced to admit that he had been given so many warnings there would be no substance for a case for Unfair Dismissal if he failed what was to be his final chance.

Tottie had stopped stroking him. He looked up to see that her head had fallen back against the cushions. Exhausted by the emotional turmoil as much as by the lateness of the hour, Tottie had fallen asleep.

Good. He slid off her lap and dropped to the floor, heading for his study. Thought they had him locked in for the night, did they? Little did *they* know the French window had a broken catch, so defective even a cat could operate it with one quick push. *Heh-heh-heh.*

Once outside, he paused and nudged the door almost shut before padding across the patio and down into the garden. Now he could get in again when he returned. If he had to return as Monty.

How odd the garden looked from this level. And smelled. And the noise! His ears twitched. The garden was alive with noise, with the traffic of insects and small nocturnal creatures. *Mice!* His whole being twitched in a sudden automatic reaction: there were mice over there!

He found himself crouching close to the ground, his eyes scanning the roots and tussocks. He noted absently that it was bright as daylight, even though the moon—and a crescent moon, at that—had gone behind a cloud. Motionless, he waited for a movement or a squeak that would betray their whereabouts.

Then it came. The tiniest of rustles. Over there! *Mice— in his garden.* He inched forward silently, planning his pounce. He'd show them!

Wait a minute! Wait a minute! Shaken, he called his wayward body back to order. There was more of Monty left in it than he had realized. *Never mind the mice, we're going to the hospital.*

Hospital . . . Firmly, he disciplined the protesting muscles, turning the reluctant body towards the right direction. The sudden mutiny of his borrowed frame had shaken him more than he was prepared to think about right now. He would have to be careful. Very careful. Who knew in what way this furry body might betray him next? He could not allow his concentration to slip for a moment; when it did, strange instincts stood ready to take over.

They would have sent Winstanley Fortescue to St Monica's Hospital. Miranda would have insisted on that. Not that she had any fond feelings for it, poor girl. It was where she had suffered out her two miscarriages. But it was also the nearest and the best. A discreet, private clinic where the social and economic status of the patients and the surrounding community precluded ambulances screaming through the night. St Monica's did not have a Casualty Department, but the standard of treatment available equalled—and sometimes surpassed—that of the best teaching hospitals.

Purposefully, he crossed the garden and squeezed through the iron bars fencing in the box hedge at the bottom. He was momentarily distracted by a familiar shape: so that was where the Terry child's guinea pig had got to. Perhaps he'd be able to tell the child . . . some day.

Sternly recalling himself to duty, he forced himself to continue on course. But, oh! the scent of the earth warming into spring, the soft ripple of the breeze through his fur, the faint fascinating sounds all around him. Could he really be hearing the buds pushing themselves up out of the softened earth? And insects skittering along subterranean passages? No wonder March hares danced in the giddiness of it all.

He breathed deeply, absorbing everything, storing it away in his conscious memory. When he got back into his own form, these new instincts and insights would add immeasurably to future performances. Many actors were able to walk catlike through a few scenes; he would be able to bring the whole living animal into his portrayal.

Crossing the street presented little problem at this hour, but the inbuilt instincts took over again and he found himself racing across at top speed. Again there was the exhilaration of the speed he reached—with no shortness of breath and plenty of speed in reserve should it be needed. How long had it been since he had felt power like that? Middle age was all very well, but intellectual achievements did not always make up for the sheer physical prowess of youth— at least, not all the time.

In his exuberance, he cantered along for several blocks, sailed effortlessly across another street, and then was brought up short by the realization that he was at the entrance to St Monica's.

What did he do now? The doors were firmly closed— with no conveniently faulty latch to allow entry. Now he missed the height, the strength, the authority that would let him stride in and demand to see Winstanley Fortescue.

He withdrew into the shadows of the bushes along the drive to consider his position.

St Monica's was housed in an imposing Victorian mansion, completely reconstructed inside to meet rigorous standards of hygiene and efficiency. Outside, the mullioned windows surrounded by luxuriant ivy gave no hint of the present purpose of the building. In fact, St Monica's was more of a private sanatorium than hospital. There was no question of treatment on the National Health; it was exclusive and expensive—and worth it because it kept its secrets well.

As he contemplated the ivy-covered façade (could he climb it? and would he find an open window if he did?) a long black limousine turned into the drive and rolled slowly up to the entrance. No sirens blaring or garish lights flashing for the advent of any of St Monica's patrons; total discretion was the watchword.

The limousine halted at the front door and a uniformed attendant leaped out and went round to lift a wheelchair out of the boot. Another man, un-uniformed and obviously a concerned relative, got out first and began making coaxing noises to someone still settled in the back seat.

'Come along, Auntie Thea, we're here. It will be nice to see your old friends again. You like this place, you know you do.'

Something sailed past his head and crashed into the gravel of the drive. An overpowering smell of liquor drifted through the air. A ringing voice declaimed what she considered suitable for an interfering nephew to do with this place—and with himself.

Well, well, well, so Dame Theodora McCarran was heading for another drying-out session, was she? He remembered reading recently that she had been signed for a feature role in a major American film to be made in this country soon. Yes, they'd have to get her into shape for that. Good luck to them!

Meanwhile, it might be a bit of luck for him. He watched as the uniformed attendant went round to the other door while Dame Theodora's attention was centred on her nephew, who was now jiggling the wheelchair invitingly and making a few more hopeful noises.

'Come along, madam.' The attendant was in the back seat, pushing Dame Theodora towards the open door.

'Take your hands off me, you miserable cretin!' the

fluting, melodious voice commanded. 'Or I'll scream "RAPE"!'

'Easy does it, Auntie Thea.' With an expertise obviously born of long practice, her nephew tilted the wheelchair to receive her as she spilled out of the car.

'That goes for you, too, you baying jackal!' His aunt rounded on him. 'Not enough guts to tread the boards yourself, like an honest cur, you bay at the heels of your betters, trying to bring them down to your level! You're a disgrace to the family, Oliver Crump!'

'If you say so, Auntie Thea.' Oliver Crump might not be an actor, but he was giving a pretty fair performance as Uriah Heep at the moment. It was easy to see who had the money in that family. 'Here now, just let me put this car rug over you to keep out the night chill.'

'Fool! Nuisance! Traitor!' Dame Theodora berated him as he tried to arrange the rug. It wound up hanging down sloppily on both sides, in danger of being entangled in the wheels. 'Take me home!'

'All in due course, Auntie Thea.' Oliver Crump turned away briefly to shut the car door. The attendant moved ahead to open the front door for them.

That was his chance! Gathering himself together, he sprang forward and raced for shelter beneath the wheelchair, where the rug drooping down on both sides would conceal his presence as they all entered St Monica's.

For once in his life, Oliver Crump was being useful.

The sensitive pads of his paws registered the changes in texture from gravel path to cement ramp and on to smooth cool linoleum smelling of floor polish and disinfectant.

There was no need to pause at the reception desk. In this sort of establishment, all arrangements were taken care of beforehand. Dame Theodora had settled into an aloof and dignified silence; Oliver Crump propelled the wheelchair straight to the lift, where he was joined by one of the nurses who introduced herself as Sister Dale, who would be Dame Theodora's personal nurse during her residence at St

Monica's. Sister Dale sportingly began a one-sided conversation with Dame Theodora, ignoring the silence that
answered her.

Together they all entered the lift and travelled upwards.
When the lift doors opened again it was to a carpeted corridor. In these upper reaches, the clinical was less important
than the soothing and opulent. Patients allotted to these
rooms were not in any immediately life-threatening situ-
ations; they were here to be cossetted, cared for and gently
reprieved from their particular addictions.

As the wheelchair halted before one of the guest suites,
he tensed again. If he bolted now, chances were that he'd
be seen; but if he entered the suite with the others, it might
not be so easy to get out again. What he needed was a
distraction. But what?

'My dear Sister Dale—' Dame Theodora roused herself
and swayed towards her nurse. 'Have you met my nephew?
The black sheep of an otherwise respectable and honoured
family.'

'Auntie Thea!' Oliver Crump protested.

'Oh, Dame Theodora,' the nurse bleated. 'You don't
mean that!'

The door swung open, the wheelchair lurched forward,
everyone talking volubly. He dived away and into the
shadows of the far corner of the corridor as they entered
the suite, each still engrossed with their own grievance. The
door swung closed behind them.

So far, so good. The Intensive Care Unit was two floors
down. He knew because Miranda had spent twenty-eight
hours there after her last miscarriage. Who would have
thought that any good might have come out of those terrible
hours?

No point in even thinking of the lift; the buttons were too
high for him to reach, even stretched to his uttermost.
Heavy fire doors shut off the emergency stairs. The main
staircase, a carved mahogany extravaganza, was exposed

to view from both above and below. If there was anyone to see who was using it.

Slinking from shadow to shadow, he hugged the wall going downstairs, freezing frequently as strange sounds assailed his quivering ears. The world was fraught with danger for a defenceless feline prowling where obtuse humans would consider he had no business to be.

One flight . . . two flights . . . then the reek of anæsthetics, medicines and nameless horrors—half-noticed when he had encountered them while in human form—almost overpowered him. He halted, panting, his lips curled back, his tongue protruding slightly between his teeth, waiting until the nausea receded and he could force himself forward again. The Intensive Care Unit was on this floor.

A current of air moved sluggishly along the corridor and the clear plastic flaps closing off the Unit quivered in the draught. There would be no difficulty getting through them; they were designed to assist entry to the Unit, not hinder it. From somewhere in the past came the memory of a medical team bursting through those flaps, pushing their life-saving trolley of supplementary emergency equipment before them.

The long flaps brushed against both flanks as he pushed through them and into the section occupied by the Intensive Care Unit, more of a cul-de-sac than a wing. There were three fully-equipped rooms for patients and a small office just inside the flaps, containing a desk, chair, lamp and telephone, where a nurse could keep vigil when the rooms were occupied.

He lowered his belly to the ground and slunk past the cubbyhole office, then realized he needn't have bothered. No one on duty there. Perhaps the nurse was attending to one of the patients, or perhaps she had left her post temporarily to look after some concern of her own.

The room directly ahead, at the end of the Unit, was empty and dark. There were patients in the other two rooms on either side of the short passageway.

He paused, listening, his fur rippling uneasily at the unsettling, unfamiliar noises emanating from both rooms. Science might be wonderful, but there were times when it seemed that Life was imitating, not Art, but a horror film. Such sound effects would not be out of place in the laboratory where the Frankenstein monster stirred slowly and creaked to life.

He slithered through the doorway on the left and came to an appalled halt.

What had they done to him?

The shrivelled body lay curled on the bed, a dried-out husk of a man. His eyes were closed, there was no colour to his skin; no breath in his lungs. He looked to be a thousand years old. Only the coldly functioning machine was keeping the semblance of life in him.

What enemy has done this to me? The cat crept forward, his fur bristling and rising, a low growl gathering in his throat.

His nose twitched. Even the scent was wrong. It wasn't just the overlay of hospital smells, ghastly though they were, there was a basic odour of . . . decay? Death?

How could that fine body of his have descended into this state so rapidly? Now that the initial shock had subsided, he moved closer and took a long cool look at the body.

It wasn't his! This was some ancient fighting his last battle, armoured by the machines. Someone else's battle. It wasn't his.

He was in the wrong room. He turned purposefully and crossed the corridor to the other room.

And there he was. Himself. His true body—from which he had been so incomprehensibly dispossessed. Lying there motionless on the stark white hospital bed. Wired up to strange machines whose display panels showed bilious green lines broken by occasional jagged peaks. Worse, there were tubes ending in sagging plastic bags that seemed to be attached to every available surface. He watched in horror as the level of amber fluid rose suddenly in the plastic bag beneath the bed.

Poor Monty must think he'd fallen into the hands of the vivisectionists . . . if it *was* Monty in there.

Could he be having one of those out-of-the-body experiences so often chronicled in the less reputable tabloids?

But in those cases the spirit self was invariably portrayed as floating around just below the ceiling and looking down on the body in the bed below. It was definitely not supposed to be firmly grounded in the body of another species strolling around at floor level. What had gone wrong?

He found the darkest shadow in the room and crouched in it, staring mournfully at the inert form on the bed. *If you have tears, prepare to shed them now.*

Unlike crocodiles, cats have no tears. The dark brooding sadness quivered through him with no outlet. A soft low dirge pulsed in his throat and he clenched his teeth against it. A race memory that was not from his own race, nor even his own species abruptly flashed through his mind: he must make no sound or they would discover him, chase him . . . harry him from the familiar hearth, from the person he loved . . .

The Instrument, they were taught to call it in the acting academies. The body, the voice, the movements—all one had to work with, but enough when properly trained and used.

The Instrument: lying there mute and still. The Instrument: could it ever be played again? Or was it destroyed for ever?

Was it lost to him—or did he still inhabit it? Was he really trapped somewhere in the depths of its coma, dreaming all that seemed to be happening to him?

He crept closer, his gaze fixed on the shuttered face. That was where he belonged—behind that blank mask, restoring it to animation, vitality . . . life.

Suppose The Instrument died? Would he be trapped here in Monty's body for the rest of his life . . . of Monty's life? And how old was Monty? No kitten, by any means. In his rackety days as a stray, he had probably used up a few of his nine lives before finding a welcome at the Stage Door and a permanent home at the Chesterton.

The Instrument had confidently assumed that another thirty-odd years stretched ahead of him. At least. There were still the great parts to be played: Falstaff, Lear, Prospero . . . And, with the life-expectancy of the current generations increasing constantly, it could not be long until the modern playwrights addressed the situation. There were many great parts waiting to be written in which ageing actors and actresses would mirror the problems and complexities facing their audience. He didn't want to miss that.

And there had been the confidence, too, that a Knighthood was in the offing. Sir Winstanley and Lady Fortescue had a magnificent ring to it; it sounded right—and was well-deserved. To think that the Powers-That-Be went through the farce of an exploratory inquiry—as though anyone in his right mind would decline the honour.

But he wasn't in his right mind. Not now. Rather, he was in his right mind, but wrong body.

As he watched, the familiar face twitched. Was that returning consciousness? Were those eyes about to open?

He advanced to the foot of the bed and crouched to spring.

Then he heard the footsteps in the corridor outside. Soft, furtive footsteps, coming closer. He changed his mind about leaping on to the bed and retreated to a corner, watching the doorway.

He was just in time. She appeared in the open doorway. *Jilly!* He shrank in on himself, trying to make himself smaller, but he need not have bothered. She had eyes for nothing except the inert form on the hospital bed.

'I knew it!' she breathed. 'I knew they were trying to keep something from me!' The gleam in her eye was disquieting as she moved swiftly to the side of the bed.

'Win,' she called urgently, but softly. 'Win, are you awake? Can you hear me?' She touched his face gently. 'Win, it's Jilly. What happened?'

There was no response. But . . . had the pattern of breathing changed slightly?

'Win—?' Her voice sharpened. She looked anxiously towards the door. 'Win, can you hear me? Can you speak?'

She'd sneaked in! Everything in her attitude betrayed that fact. Well, so had he. And she was afraid of getting caught, too. This was where it was an advantage to be a cat; they'd simply sweep him out the door if they caught him. Jilly would have some tricky explaining to do.

Very tricky. Even as he watched, she backed away from the bed, then circled it slowly, noting every tube and wire.

'Win—?' She was testing this time, before she went further. And this time she seemed satisfied at receiving no response. She nodded and approached the bedside again.

After a final searching glance at the still face, she pulled back the sheet and folded it away from the unconscious body.

Had a man no privacy at all? He quivered with outrage as she then lifted the hospital gown and brazenly peered underneath it.

How right Miranda had been to refuse to talk to Jilly! How wise. Dear Miranda . . . a melancholy swept over him. He had never appreciated her enough. How could he make it up to her?

There was an explosive hiss of exultation from Jilly. She had found something that meant something to her. But nothing meant anything to Jilly except a story. He knew that now.

What had she found? He crept forward; he had to know. But her body blocked his view. She was leaning forward, inspecting some portion of The Instrument normally kept decently covered.

Damn the consequences! He leapt for the bed. She couldn't complain; she was here illegally, too.

It all happened at once: Jilly smothered a scream. The eyes of the inert figure opened and he stared uncomprehendingly at Jilly.

'Win, darling—you're awake!'

Then he saw Monty. He stretched out towards the cat, his body thrashing with the uncoordinated movements of someone who did not know how to control the strange appendages he found at his command. As he lurched for the cat, tubes and wires rocked violently, the patterns on the monitor screen went berserk, high-pitched electronic bleeps gave the alarm that would bring the emergency medical team running.

'Hell!' Jilly backed away; the cat leaped back to the floor. He didn't reckon his chances if an Instrument operated by Monty got him in its clutches.

Outside, running footsteps cut off any hope of escape in that direction. Jilly looked around wildly. There was no place to hide in the room.

She dashed for the window and threw it open, hurling herself into the ivy and hoping it would hold. The cat was right behind her. Together they scrabbled down to the ground.

'You rotten little sod!' Jilly snarled as they landed in the flowerbed. 'You ruined everything. I could kill you!'

Equally furious, he glared back at her before turning and running into the bushes. *She'd* like to kill him? Didn't she understand what she had seen?

The proof that someone else had already tried.

8

Because of the telephone call, Miranda was late for the meeting. The others were already assembled on stage, in chairs spread out across the length of the stage, as though for a first read-through. The stagehands had pushed the partly-constructed scenery back against the wall and were standing beside it, watching the others and waiting.

Antoinette was there, wearing a black-and-white outfit

that made her look more like a magpie than the ex-wife in semi-mourning she so obviously intended. Jennet was beside her (surely, it was unnecessary to drag the child away from school for this?), looking ill at ease and wary. There was an empty chair on the other side of Antoinette, but Geoffrey had had the good sense to distance himself. He was at the far side of the stage, talking to Peter Farley, frowning portentously, projecting 'two men deep in vitally important conversation' and avoiding his mother's increasingly furious eye as she tried to signal him to her side.

Some women didn't deserve to have children! Antoinette was using her children as stage dressing for whatever part she had cast herself in, the better to manipulate everyone's emotions.

'Miranda.' Davy came forward and took her hand, leading her to the empty chair centre stage. 'Any news?'

'The hospital rang—that's why I'm late. Win . . . rallied, but only briefly. They don't know whether it's a good sign or not . . .'

Being cautious, they thought not. They had tried to discourage any hope on her part with their bleak medical vocabulary. *Brain stem . . . motor responses . . . vital signs . . . automatic reflexes . . .*

She became aware that everyone had gone quiet, shamelessly eavesdropping, and she pitched her voice accordingly. It was not the sort of information one wished to keep repeating. Let them all hear it now.

'He seems to have slipped back into the coma again.'

A murmur of sympathy swept the stage and reached out to enfold her. Comforting concerned glances were directed at her, silently assuring her of love and support. They were all on her side—and Win's.

Or were they? Suddenly she was aware of a violent jolt of emotion flashing through the atmosphere. Someone was neither concerned nor supportive. Someone was seething with repressed rage and hostility. Someone was furious at the thought that Win might still stand a chance of recovery. But who?

The obvious ill-wisher was Antoinette. Curiously, the hostility did not seem to be emanating from her—at least, not any more than usual. Antoinette sat with eyes downcast —except when she beamed fury at the son who was not playing the game by sitting on her other side in support of his grieving and hard-done-by mother. Beside her, young Jennet looked increasingly embarrassed and terrified.

Abruptly, Miranda recognized the role Antoinette was playing: the grieving widow at the reading of the will.

But Antoinette was merely the ex-wife and Win was not dead. Not yet. Not at all, if medical science and the experts Miranda had commanded to his side had anything to do with it.

But . . . had anyone else had anything to do with it? For the first time, she questioned the circumstances of Win's fall, forcing herself to remember . . .

It had been one of those fragmented rehearsals, with Rufus going from one cast member to another, blocking out movements which would later be integrated into the ensemble scene leading to the first act curtain. Davy was by his side, taking notes.

The setting was a drawing-room in Victorian Edinburgh on Christmas Eve. Win, as paterfamilias, had just led his brood home from some festivity in the town, which meant that they were wearing full evening dress. Miranda played his new young wife; Geoffrey, his son by his dear-departed first wife; Cynthia, his sister, who knew all the family secrets; and Peter Farley, a mysterious American friend of Cynthia's who had somehow insinuated himself into the family gathering.

Serpent in the Heather was loosely based on a little-known nineteenth-century Edinburgh poisoning case. The author had taken his oath that there were no descendants still alive who might make trouble—and then left for a Hollywood scripting assignment, promising to return for the First Night.

The key scene was that first act curtain. Having returned in high spirits (in every sense of the words), Win decided it was time to trim the Christmas tree.

The battle was still on—had been on—*was* still on, as to whether Win should be wearing a kilt or tartan trews. Needless to say, Win favoured trews; Rufus insisted a kilt was the only proper formal attire, especially with that ruffled, lace-cuffed shirt. It was Win's contention that the front rows were getting enough value for money without a peep up his skirts as well, as he mounted the stepladder to place the star on top of the Christmas tree.

To help decide the issue, Tottie had run up a practice kilt for Win to wrap over his trousers. Eddie, Bob and Woody, the stagehands who were working in a welter of poles and trellis slats as they cannibalized an old rose arbour set into the conservatory opening off the drawing-room, had sportingly donated an eight-foot pole. Win had crammed the pole into an umbrella stand already full of umbrellas and walking sticks which he had commandeered from the star dressing-room to stand in for the huge Christmas tree that would dominate the finished set.

Win had then experimented with various ways of going up and down the stepladder; dashing up, skipping up, with a jaunty air, with a thoughtful air, soberly and not so soberly—with a careful eye to the disposition of his kilt with each varying movement.

The others had been busy with their own several parts: Miranda was engaging in a delicate flirtation with Peter Farley; Cynthia was quietly expiring in a corner from the effects of a poison administered by persons unknown at a time unknown; and Geoffrey was torn between a sudden anxiety about his aunt and the demands of his father who kept requiring various ornaments to be passed to him to trim the tree.

They had all had their backs to Win when the accident happened.

But it was not the first time Win had been darting up and down the stepladder. He was as sure-footed as a cat, with no trace of faltering or awkwardness; his only uncertainty had been about the kilt.

Why, then, had he fallen off?

Perhaps they ought to check the stepladder to see if anyone might have put grease on one of the steps. It might have been intended as a joke, but it had been misjudged and produced dire consequences. If that were so, naturally no one was going to admit to it now. Pranksters abounded in the theatre; in fact, Geoffrey had been rather notorious for practical jokes in his very recent teenage years. Until Win had read the Riot Act to him. Had Geoffrey done some backsliding and thought it would be hilarious to play a trick that would undermine his father's dignity and authority?

No . . . probably not. Thoughtfully, she exonerated Geoffrey. Like his father, he was theatre through and through. He would have done nothing to jeopardize the production —and he would have realized that a fall would bring the risk of a sprained ankle or broken bone, if nothing worse. Injury to the star would have meant the postponement, or even cancellation, of the play. And this play was Geoffrey's big chance. A plum role, opposite his own father, giving him a chance to show his paces. No, Geoffrey would have done nothing to blow this chance.

Antoinette, however, wouldn't care about the production. Not if she had a chance to get at Win. And one needn't work in the theatre—or be present at all—to arrange for an accident. She had already dropped in several times to visit Geoffrey when Win wasn't around. No one would have thought anything of it if she'd wandered about a bit, looking at the stage setting, the props . . . and what else?

She could not be sure that Win would fall into her trap —or that it would be fatal. Perhaps she didn't care whether it was or not. She might simply have wanted to hurt and upset him. On the other hand, she might have been acting with extreme malice—and she might have set a number of other traps in case the first one didn't have the desired effect.

But again, there was the question: would Antoinette have jeopardized her son's future just to get some sort of revenge on her ex-husband? And, if she carried that deep a grudge, why hadn't she done something about it before now?

'All right, everybody,' Rufus Tuxford said. 'Shall we settle down and have our meeting?'

Geoffrey reluctantly assumed his place at his mother's side. The stagehands ranged themselves along the back of the set. The murmur of voices died away and faces turned expectantly to the producer.

'First of all,' Rufus said, 'I know we all want to extend our utmost sympathy to Miranda—'

Antoinette sniffed.

'And to Jennet and Geoffrey,' he added hurriedly. 'And, er, Antoinette.'

Miranda restrained a sniff of her own. She settled for a patient forgiving smile which made Rufus wince.

'Right, the next question I know you all want the answer to is: what's going to happen to the show?'

A murmur of agreement rose from the assembly. Anxious faces, trying not to look too anxious, watched him, waiting.

'Right. As you know, I've been holding informal discussions and the general agreement is that The Show Must Go On. Miranda . . . ?' This time it was his face that was anxious as he turned to her.

'Yes, of course,' she agreed, knowing how much the answer would mean to the others. 'If we can . . .'

'We're still in the early stages of rehearsal. Cynthia and Peter have been doubling as understudies for you and Win. I'm glad to say that Peter is willing and able to step in— until Win can rejoin the cast.'

Peter Farley nodded, keeping up the fiction that Win had

nothing more serious wrong with him than a couple of broken bones and needed nothing more than a short convalescence.

'And . . .' Rufus hesitated. 'You'll stay with us, Miranda, playing your own part?'

Miranda took a deep breath and nodded. What else could she do? She'd go mad without something to keep her busy. She couldn't just hang about waiting to see if Win rallied again. And, from what the doctors had been trying to put across to her delicately, if he *did* begin to recover, it could be a long process. Long and expensive. They would need all the money she could earn. She had to keep on working.

'Good! We might be able to arrange a short provincial tour before bringing it into the West End. That would give Win a bit more time to recover.'

And it would also give Peter Farley more time to work himself into the part. This was a big opportunity for him. And he needed one. Stepping into the leading part would make all the difference to him now that he was rebuilding his life in England.

Peter had been rising steadily in his career when he met and married a girl from Texas and returned with her to that State. He had carved out a comfortable niche for himself in a repertory company there and done well for several years until the marriage broke up. Packing his bags and a few souvenirs, he had returned to London to find himself almost forgotten and a whole new wave of young talent competing for the few jobs available. He'd tightened his belt and begun doing the rounds.

But the West End isn't particularly kind to those who have abandoned it for pastures which turned out to be not so much greener, after all. The returning prodigal was expected to re-apprentice himself, start almost at the beginning again—with too many years lost and no guarantee of eventual success.

Peter's ability to slide into an American accent had won him the part in *Serpent in the Heather*. His willingness to double as understudy also helped. And now that he was stepping into the leading role, he would reap far more publicity than he normally would have. The media would flock to what was already being called 'The Fortescue Family Play' to see how it would fare without the senior Fortescue. It would showcase Peter Farley as nothing else could.

'Oh, Rufus,' Cynthia called. 'Who's going to do Peter's part now? Do you have any ideas?' She sounded as though she might, if he didn't.

'I'm going to try for Jack Long,' Rufus said. 'I've heard he'd like to take a leave of absence from that Soap and get some more stage experience. He'll be great—and we'll have the added bonus of the audience he'll attract.'

'Oh . . . fine,' Cynthia said. 'He should be all right.'

'Right!' Rufus exuded relief. Evidently he had been more anxious than he appeared, but now that everyone was responding as he had wished, he was fully in command again. 'Then we'll start rehearsing Peter right away. Geoffrey, if you'd stay and run through the scenes with him . . . ?'

'Of course,' Geoffrey said.

'Geoffrey, I want you to come with me to see your father!' Antoinette's voice cracked like a whip. 'He should have his *family* around his bedside at a time like this.'

'I'm not sure Win is allowed visitors,' Miranda murmured.

'Nonsense! They can't keep *us* out! We have the *right* to be there. You can't stop us.'

'I wouldn't dream of trying to stop you,' Miranda said. She would let St Monica's take care of that.

9

He had fallen asleep suddenly and against all his intentions, but now he was awake and trying to convince himself that he was really awake, properly awake. In the early days of their marriage, Antoinette had fallen under the influence of the first of a series of gurus. It had been very much the fashion then and he had not known enough to mark it as the beginning of her increasing instability. For a while, he had gone along with her to various meetings and had even been given a mantra of his own, which he occasionally muttered under emotional duress.

He had devised a new mantra now: *I am Winstanley Fortescue, a star, at the height of my powers and my profession. When I open my eyes, I will be home in bed, awaking from a nightmare. I am Winstanley Fortescue . . .*

He opened his eyes. He was still under the bushes on the grounds of St Monica's. Worse, he was cold and hungry. And it was going to rain. Any minute. He knew it. He no longer questioned how he knew such things. He just did. It came with the territory—this strange furry territory he inhabited.

That was what had wakened him: the knowledge of the impending storm and the instinct to find better shelter. He would not have time to reach home before the storm broke. The Chesterton Theatre was even farther away. He allowed himself to reach the decision he had already made:

He had to get back inside St Monica's. Back to himself.

He studied the building. A clump of torn-away ivy marked the window he and Jilly had tumbled through, but the window was firmly closed now. So was the front door. He was unlikely to have a repeat of the sort of luck that had allowed him to slip in with the new patient last night. And the darkness had helped.

The bushes rustled above him as the first large raindrops fell. A chill wind eddied along the ground, rippling his fur. He rose hastily, stretched and gathered himself together for the dash across the open lawn to the shelter of the over-hanging eaves.

The back door. The kitchen. The knowledge came to him unbidden. Pressing close to the building, he followed the sweep of red brick and ivy. The smell of food grew stronger as he rounded the corner and became the magnet that drew him on.

Chicken! They were cooking chicken! He loved chicken! A faint plaintive yowl rose in his throat as, everything else forgotten, he stopped at the back door and stared up at it long-ingly. From the cracks around and beneath the door, delicious smells seeped out. His stomach contracted with hunger.

Yes, it was probably creamed chicken on the menu tonight. He had gathered from Miranda that creamed chicken appeared on the menu with monotonous regularity, partly because so many of the patients were in for various abdominal operations and partly because certain of the other patients were not to be trusted with knives. The strength of their complaints about the menu was a measure of their progress towards recovery. Silly people. Creamed chicken seemed like heaven to him right now.

How could he get at it? Earlier in the day there might have been deliveries coming to the back door, but it was too late for that now. No chance of slipping in with an unwary tradesperson.

The window-sill was an easy leap and gave an enticing view into the kitchen. The big Aga held a variety of pots and pans with steam rising from each of them. A salmon was poaching in a long low utensil; now that he had seen it, he could differentiate that scent from the others. Delicious, all of them, delicious. His stomach contracted again.

He pressed closer against the window-pane, strange little

plaintive yodelings escaping his throat. He could not seem to find the control mechanism to stop the sounds. Monty had always been a great vocalist, he recalled.

A sudden gust of wind slammed a downpour of rain against the window-sill and all over him. He gave an involuntary yowl of protest.

The woman bending over the stove straightened and her head turned. He crouched lower on the window-sill, but could not stop the now-hopeful yowl coming from his throat. The woman looked so pleasant, so kind—and there was something delicious dripping from the ladle in her hand . . . She saw him and moved forward.

'Now what are you doing out there?' She raised the window and he tumbled into the warmth and fragrance of the kitchen, purring loudly.

'I'll get in trouble if they catch you in here, you know that?' The thought did not appear to trouble her unduly. He breathed deeply and found himself winding ingratiatingly around her ankles. Why should she worry? Anyone who could cook like this could write her own ticket.

'Now stop that—you're getting me all wet. Let me dry you off and then we'll find you some scraps.'

He forced himself to remain quiet as she wrapped paper towels around him, blotting the excessive moisture. Her hands and her clothing were impregnated with cooking smells. What a delightful woman!

'All right, we'll get you something to eat now.' He followed her as she found a cereal bowl and filled it with savoury titbits.

'Over here.' She placed it on the floor, against the wall and beside the stove. 'Now, if anybody comes in, you go and hide behind the Aga or we'll both be in trouble—and they'll throw *you* out. All right?'

He headbutted her ankle gently, wishing he had a clearer way of telling her he understood. He would not get this charming woman into trouble for the world—nor did he wish to be thrown back out into the storm. As soon as he had cleared this bowl, he had things to do in this building. He had to check and see how Monty was coming along.

But first, perhaps he could persuade her to give him a second helping . . .

He felt the floor quiver under the steady silent advance of the firm authoritative tread. *Trouble!* He just knew. He lifted the remaining chuck of chicken from his bowl and retreated behind the stove with it.

Just in time. The now-audible steps crossed the kitchen and he heard the thump of someone subsiding heavily into a chair at the table, then a long-drawn-out sigh.

'Playing up, is she?' the cook asked sympathetically.

'They usually do, at this stage.' Sister Dale's voice was resigned. 'Sober and sulking. Bored out of her mind and furious. That idiot nephew of hers forgot to bring along her glasses, so she can't read, can't do a jigsaw puzzle, can't even focus properly on the television. I shouldn't like to be in his shoes next time he comes to visit.'

Poor Thea. She didn't deserve the relatives she had. No wonder she occasionally took refuge in a bottle.

'Never mind, she'll enjoy her salmon. It's almost ready.'

'Yes, and I've rung the nephew and left a message for him to send round her glasses as soon as possible. I hope he does it right away. She's getting very restless.'

'And we all know what that means.' There was the sound of liquid pouring; tea was evidently being taken. 'Never a quiet moment here when we have theatricals. At least the other one is still out of action, isn't he?'

'More or less.' There was a frown in the voice. 'His relatives and friends are more trouble than he is. There's a constant procession. We have to keep turning them away, but I wouldn't trust them not to sneak in. Someone did last night. *And* left the window open with the wind blowing in on him. Doctor already suspects a slight bronchial infection. He's not pleased. Between that and Sir Reginald Peyton, the patient's own physician, flying back from the States, he can't do the exploratory operation he wants to do.'

Operation? Exploratory? Abruptly, his fur stood on end, his tail bushed, his mouth opened in a soundless hiss. He crept forward, pushing his head clear of the great bulk of the cooker. He didn't want to miss anything.

'I don't know, I just don't like those exploratories.' Again, the cook proved herself a peerless woman of extreme sensibility. 'It doesn't seem right to open a head when there's nothing wrong with it, just to poke around inside.'

'But there *is* something wrong with it. The brainwave patterns are registering a disorder. We've got to find out what it is.'

'I don't hold with it. The poor man ought to be left in peace while he recovers naturally. He got awfully knocked about and it isn't as though he's in a real deep coma. You said he halfway came out of it last night.'

'Yes, and I'm not so sure he sank back into it. Oh, he's lying there motionless all right, but somehow I just don't believe it.'

Good old Monty. He recognized the cat's favourite stratagem. When you don't know what to do, go to sleep. Or pretend to sleep.

'I'd like to be able to keep a closer watch over him, but I can't spare the time. If only we weren't so short-handed at present.'

'It's this 'flu epidemic, dear. Half of London is down with it. I've only Sally to help in the kitchen because of it—and I've had to send her to the shops. It's going to have to be bottled Hollandaise tonight, I've no time to bother making it with everything else I've got to do.'

'We're all on overload.' There was the scrape of a chair being pushed back. 'I've got to try ringing round again and see if we can get some Agency nurses in. Matron had to send Lesley and Henry home before they collapsed—or, worse, infected the patients. That means there's no one on Reception. Oh dear.' She sighed deeply.

'Never mind, we'll be back to normal in a few days. We can manage until then.'

'I suppose so.' The white shoes marched across the room and out the door. He listened attentively, following their progress down the hallway, up the stairs and into the office behind the reception desk. The coast was clear.

He slipped out from behind the stove and started for the door.

'No! Don't go up there!' the voice called out behind him. 'No! Bad cat! Come back!' Rapid footsteps advanced on him, he could feel hands reaching out for him.

He sprang for the stairs and raced upwards.

10

Was it because he had been here before in this new incarnation that the long staircase seemed less threatening and dangerous? Or was it that there was something vaguely familiar and reassuring about it? He crouched in the shadows of the first landing and took a few experimental sniffs. There was something in the air . . . well-known scents . . . a trace of greasepaint . . . a hint of brandy . . . an exotic tobacco . . .

He found that his nose could read the scents as surely as his eyes had once read newspapers: friends were here, or had been here, visiting him. Rather, visiting an uncomprehending Monty.

He dashed up the remaining steps at renewed speed. It was probably all right while Monty was still pretending sleep, but what if he decided to open his eyes and try to make contact? The smells, voices and faces would be just as familiar to him; he would know that he was among friends. But had he yet realized what had happened to him?

He slid through the swinging plastic flaps and around the corner, restraining his impulse to burst into the room. A grand entrance would not be appreciated in a cat. He noted absently that he was developing a nice line in slinks.

But the room was empty, except for the motionless body on the hospital bed. Eyes closed, machine-assisted breathing regular, it appeared unaware of its surroundings. Yet the additional senses he had acquired along with his furry body told him that the human body was both conscious and concerned. Puzzled, worried and frightened, it lay there . . . waiting for something that it could understand.

The fragrance of Miranda still hung in the air. He could remember the day he bought it for her . . . and the extortionate price . . . and the afternoon with Cynthia which was the reason he had been willing to pay that price. Mmmm, perhaps some things were best not dwelt upon.

Miranda had been here. Recently. Dear Miranda. She loved that perfume.

It had been such a success that he had also purchased, despite the price, a small flagon of it for Jennet. (Yes, he felt guilty about that poor little last-throw-to-save-the-marriage daughter, too. The marriage hadn't lasted beyond her third birthday.) Jennet had loved the perfume, but complained that her mother helped herself to it frequently and lavishly, pointing out that it was too mature a scent for so young a girl.

His hackles rose abruptly. Was it possible that it had not been Miranda in here, but Antoinette? Come to see for herself how the mighty were fallen? To gloat? It would be just the sort of thing she'd do.

And there was another odour in the air . . . something unpleasant. The smell of enmity, but not Antoinette's. Someone else had been here who was not a friend. Instinctively, he lowered his head and began to inhale deeply, his mouth opening slightly, as though to taste the smell.

It led him to the baseboard running around the room. It was especially heavy by the electrical socket right by the door. As though someone had stood there for some time, perhaps contemplating the array of plugs supplying power to the life-saving machines servicing the body.

'*Pull the plug,*' he had heard Rufus say to Tottie. Had someone been thinking of doing just that?

A low growl welled up in his throat, his claws flexed. Someone standing here staring at that helpless body, invading its privacy with their gloating eyes. Then looking down at the plug . . . If he caught them, he'd have torn them apart with his bare teeth and claws.

Hold it! Hold it! He shook himself, letting the fur fall back into place. The Monty responses were taking over again, feline to the core, battling the alien brain fighting to control them. What was happening in that body on the bed? Did the instincts and motor responses of Winstanley Fortescue lie there intact, waiting only for the cues that would set them in motion?

Will the real Monty please stand up? Will the real Winstanley Fortescue please stand up? If only they could.

Steady on now! He throttled down on the forlorn wail his throat wanted to give vent to. *Emotion will get us nowhere. This situation calls for brainpower. And luck.*

Suddenly that preternatural hearing alerted him: there were footsteps coming along the corridor outside. People were heading this way.

Just before he dived for the shelter of the shadows in the farthest corner of the room, he saw the eyes of The Instrument open in the narrowest of cat's-slits. Monty's mind was also sentient and alert. There *must* be a way of reaching it, communicating with it . . . exchanging with it.

He huddled in the corner, tucking his tail in tightly around his body, crouching low to diminish the gleaming expanse of white shirtfront fur. As the footsteps came closer, he ducked his head and his own eyes narrowed. Whoever it was, they were definitely heading for this room—and the nurse was not with them.

'*Shhh* . . .' Jilly's head craned around the door frame as she stopped outside and carefully reconnoitred the territory before moving forward. 'All clear. Come along, Jake, quickly! We can't be sure how long we'll have the place to ourselves.'

A large male figure lumbered into the room behind her. It was draped with camera equipment and the camera itself.

Finger to her lips, Jilly motioned him to the far side of the bed, then approached the bed herself.

'Win . . . ? Win . . . ?' Her voice was soft and cooing; a tone not many people heard. There were some people who would be prepared to swear that it was impossible for her to sound so gentle and concerned.

'Win . . . ?' She stroked the face lightly, watching for any sign of response. But . . . had there always been that slightly false note in her cooing tone?

'Win . . . ?' This time she tapped his face, not quite a slap, but with a certain amount of force. 'Win . . . can you hear me? Move your fingers if you can.'

The body remained motionless, even the narrow glittering slit that had betrayed the watching eyes had disappeared. The eyes were firmly closed, there was no flicker of response.

'Right! He's still out. Set up fast. Let's get our pictures and get out of here.'

'Don't rush me,' Jake said. 'It's not often I get a subject who isn't running in the opposite direction the minute he sees my camera. I want to do full justice to this; there could be a small fortune in syndication rights. Move out of the way—I want a clear shot of all the medical equipment in the background.' He began fiddling with the camera.

In the corner, the cat hissed silently. He watched as Jilly circled the bed again, looking at the supine form with cold dispassion. He had thought she cared . . . at least a little bit. How could she behave like this? Betray him by exhibiting his helpless condition to the readers of her filthy rag?

Light flashed several times in rapid succession. The photographer lowered the camera and moved to a new position, literally covering every angle.

'Get the establishing shots,' Jilly urged him on, a faint nervousness in her voice. 'Then we'll go for the nitty-gritty.'

'Just a few more . . .' Jake crouched and shot, moved to the foot of the bed and shot again, then seemed to take several more shots at random. 'You know, I think he moved a bit just then.'

'Win . . . ?' Jilly was instantly wary. She moved forward apprehensively. 'Win . . . ? Are you . . . are you . . . *there?*'

The body wanted to move, to protest. He could feel it. His ears twitched in sympathy.

'It's all right.' Jilly moved out of camera range again. 'He's still out. Just think.' She gave a short sharp laugh. 'It may be the old ham's last photo call—and he isn't conscious to enjoy it.'

Old? Ham? She hadn't talked like that when they were passing Cartier's! He growled softly. It was probably too late to stop the cheque—even if he were in any position to do so.

And . . . *last photo call?* The rest of her remarks registered. How much did she know? Were they really planning to pull the plug? Would Miranda allow it?

'I hate all these weird noises.' Jake lowered his camera and frowned at the bank of medical equipment. 'They're really spooking me. I've got enough now, can't we get out of here?'

'One last shot. The big one.' Jilly advanced purposefully to the side of the bed. 'Get ready . . . you'll have to grab it fast. I'll need to turn him on his side for it—and that may start the alarms going again.'

'What do you mean—"again"? What alarms? Jesus!' Jake flinched as she stripped the sheet from the recumbent form. 'Be careful!'

'Just you be ready to get the shot when I heave him over.' Jilly grasped the shoulders and took a long measuring look at the various points where the machines and tubes were attached. 'I'll do it without disturbing the connections if I can, but I won't promise anything.'

He could feel the waves of panic from poor Monty, feel the wild impulse to run away and climb a tree. But the body was pinned and anchored by the needles and tubes, clamps and wires; he was a prisoner in strange territory, in an unfamiliar body.

'Right.' Jake aimed the camera and stood waiting. 'Whenever you're ready.'

'Here we go . . .' Jilly gritted her teeth and slowly heaved the body over. So far, so good. He was almost on his side without dislodging any of the wires or tubes. She fumbled for the fastenings on his hospital gown and undid them, pulling the cloth away from his back.

'There! Can you get that?'

Yes! It was there as he'd seen it the first time, as he remembered it. A dark violent bruise in the middle of his back.

'Jesus!' The photographer whistled; the camera flashed. 'What happened to him?'

'That's the question I'm going to lead off with.' Jilly was panting slightly with the effort of holding Win in position —he was no lightweight, but it was worth it.

'DID HE FALL? OR WAS HE PUSHED?' Jilly quoted her proposed headlines with relish. 'THE PUBLIC DEMANDS TO KNOW!'

'That's a great story all right.' The camera flashed several times. 'The only thing that could improve it would be if the old boy died. Then we could demand a murder investigation.'

'Hurry up, I can't hold him much longer.' Win was beginning to slip from her grasp.

'OK.' The camera flashed a final time, then Jake leaped to her side. 'I've got him. Lower him easy now. We don't want to jar any of those tubes out.'

'He . . . he seems to have gone rigid.' There was a quiver in Jilly's voice, as well there might be. 'Do you think we've jiggled something the wrong way? Maybe one of those

feeder tubes is sending too much of something into him—
or too little.'

'*You* were doing all the jiggling.' Jake backed away
hastily.

'Never mind that.' Jilly started for the door. 'We've got
what we came for. Let's get out of here.'

'You're not going to leave him like that?' Jake was
shocked.

'Like what?' Jilly frowned at him uncomprehendingly.
'He's in the hands of the doctors. There's nothing I can
do.'

'No, I mean—' He broke off and gestured helplessly,
seeing that he was misunderstood. It was quicker to do it
himself. He stepped forward and draped the sheet back
over the body, covering it decently. 'That's what I meant.'

Someone was coming. More than one . . . His ears caught
the resonances on the stairs. There was something familiar
about the sounds. He lifted his head, questing for a scent
on the vagrant air currents.

'Someone's coming!' Now that they were closer, Jilly
heard the footsteps, too. 'You've wasted time fooling
around—' She turned her fury on her colleague. 'And now
our escape route is blocked off.'

'We can't go down—but we can go up!' Jake grabbed
her arm and hurried her through the door.

He could trace the pattern of footsteps (what ears Monty
had!) as the sets narrowly missed each other. One set walking normally, advancing from below; the other set on tiptoes
and rushing upwards to the floor above, gaining it before
the lower set reached the Intensive Care Unit.

Jilly and Jake were safely away.

11

He was not. He looked around wildly for a hiding-place as the realization dawned on him. It was all very well to huddle in a corner when two egomaniacs completely wrapped up in their own concerns were concentrating only on the unfortunate subject who was to be another stepping stone in their careers, but proper visitors had a way of looking around the room to check that everything possible was being done to ensure the comfort and care of their loved one. He had done it himself when visiting Miranda. Also, it gave an excuse for occasionally looking away from the tearstained face, or, in this case, the motionless form.

The bedside cabinet. It was not strictly at the bedside, it had been pushed aside to allow room for the equipment. Nor was there any need for the carafe of water, paper tissues, pills and usual accoutrements cluttering the top. The patient was beyond wanting or needing anything at this stage; if the situation improved, the cabinet would be replaced. Meanwhile, it stood inconspicuously against the wall, the little locker door below the shelves just slightly ajar.

In an instant he had pried it open and slid inside. Cursing his clumsy claw and paw, he was not able to pull the door completely shut. Perhaps that was just as well, he wanted to be able to see out.

Not that there was much to see. Life at floor level inclined towards the boring. No wonder cats had these extra senses in compensation, or that they preferred to spend so much time on chairs and table-tops. Ankles were not the most expressive portions of the human anatomy.

'OOoooh . . .' He heard Tottie's soft intake of breath as she entered the room.

'He's not as bad as he looks,' Miranda said fiercely. 'He'll come out of this. Look, Burt, his colour is better already.'

'That's right.' There was a false note in their agent's voice, he sounded as though he were deciding how quickly he could make his excuses and leave. 'You're looking fine, Win, old chap. Ha-ha, you had us worried for a bit there. Ought to be ashamed of yourself, upsetting everyone like that.'

'Win, love—' he sensed that Tottie had taken one of his hands. 'You're going to be all right. Your friends are here. We're going to take care of you.'

'Win . . .' Miranda had taken his other hand. 'Win, the doctors say they can't be sure whether you can hear us or not. I *know* you can. Don't worry. We're here; we're going to stay here. I'm setting up a roster—all your friends are going to come and visit you and talk to you. You're not alone, you're not forgotten . . .'

'That's right, old chap,' Burt said. 'You're not going to get a moment's peace. Miranda has rounded up everyone you've ever met. They're going to come round and bore you until you bounce out of that coma in sheer self-defence.' His voice was too hearty, he didn't believe a word he was saying. But Miranda was still a fee-paying client, even if Win had to be written off.

'We'll pull you through, Win,' Tottie said. 'You can depend on us. We won't let them—' She broke off abruptly.

'We're here, Win,' Miranda said firmly. 'We're staying here. You don't have to worry about a thing. Just concentrate on getting better. We'll take care of everything else.'

Dear Miranda, she was a fighter. He felt a purr of approval well up in his throat. It was not always easy living with a fighter but, when you were down and out, that was just what you needed on your side. Dear Miranda, bless her.

'What's happened to Antoinette?' Burt looked around. 'I thought she was coming over here with Geoffrey and Jennet. I expected to find them here ahead of us.'

'Been and gone,' Tottie said. 'I had a word with Reception downstairs. Her Ladyship came in, took one look, and treated herself to fine fit of hysterics. Well, it's one way to make sure the kids concentrate on her and not on Win, isn't it? She never could stand not being the centre of attention. They had to take her away and calm her down. She said she might be back later—but not if that nurse knows it.'

Bless dear Tottie, too. She was a smart woman. Lovely woman . . . warm . . . friendly . . . understanding . . . and always with some tasty nibbles cached away for her friend, Monty . . .

Damn! He caught himself inching forward and stopped. Monty's instincts had caught him off guard and were taking over again.

The disquieting question occurred to him again: what was happening to his own instincts inside that motionless body?

'Win, darling—' Miranda's voice broke. 'Come back to me!'

This time his own reaction had him half way out of the locker before he could stop himself. That would never do. She wouldn't understand. Worse, she would only see a cat whose hairs might pollute the antiseptic atmosphere of a sickroom. They would take him away, back to the house or the theatre.

He would not be able to keep watch over his property— his Instrument.

Miranda was quietly sobbing now. Tottie was making vague little noises of distress. The machinery pinged, hummed and blipped, quietly getting on with its business of sustaining life.

'Come along,' Burt said. 'I'll take you home. You need to rest. This has been a great strain on you.'

'That's right,' Tottie said. 'You go along. I'll take the first shift here. I've brought along the script of *Safe Harbour*, his first big success. I'll sit here and read it to him. That ought to get through to him, if anything can. I wouldn't be surprised if he sat up in bed and began speaking the dialogue along with me.'

'Thank you, Tottie.' There were kiss-kiss sounds. 'You're a darling. Geoffrey should be along about midnight to take over from you.'

'No problem if he isn't. I've sat up often enough with sick children in my time. It won't worry me to lose my beauty sleep.'

She walked to the door with them and came back alone. There was the scrape of a chair.

'Now then,' she said. 'Act one, Scene One, the curtain rises on you sitting on a quay in your white Aran sweater. Remember? The audience was silent. That was the last time they didn't applaud when they saw you. And that white Aran sweater became all the rage that season—and the next. Everyone took to wearing them, but they didn't look the way you did in one. A young god, that was you . . .'

Yes, yes, he remembered. Lulled by the soft rhythm of her voice, soothed by the memories of triumph past, he found himself relaxing. His eyes closed. Just for a moment, he promised himself. Just for a moment . . .

'I was in that play, you know. Sometimes I wonder if you remember that . . .' Something in Tottie's tone jerked him back to full, wary consciousness.

'Do you remember, Win—or would you rather forget?' There was a long pause and he knew that she was staring at The Instrument.

'I played your little sister. The one who died in Act Two and you went on to avenge in Act Three. It was my first major role . . . the only one, as it turned out. Remember, Win?

'Ah, would you remember, even if you could? I'll never forget it, of course. I thought it was the beginning of great things. Silly of me, wasn't it? How we deceive ourselves . . .'

Did she still remember that? They had never mentioned it when they met again years later. He thought she hadn't minded . . . not too much. After all, she'd been happily

married and starting a family. Whereas he had only recently begun going with Antoinette and the temptation to
have her acting in the same play . . .

'I was still a bride . . . well, practically. I'd no idea I was
going to fall pregnant so fast. We wanted the baby, but I
also wanted my career. How many girls have been ship-
wrecked on that reef?

'I stayed with the show right up into the fifth month—
but you weren't very happy about it, I could tell. It frightened you, I think. That scene where you had to pick me up
and swing me around—it wasn't just that I was getting
heavier. You were afraid you might do some damage, or
that you might drop me.

'The Management dropped me, in the end. Oh, they told
me I could come back into the part after the baby arrived.
And you promised it, too; even though I knew you wanted
the part for your new girlfriend, I believed you. But it never
happened. Antoinette was a big hit in the part and they
weren't going to take it away from her and give it back to
me, no matter what they'd said.

'Oh, perhaps it was just as well,' Tottie sighed. 'Pat
didn't really want me to go on working; he was earning
plenty. And it seemed as though the next baby arrived right
on the heels of the first. So I didn't mind all that much . . .
not then.

'But after Pat died so suddenly, I needed the money. I'd
have liked to go back on stage, too. Oh, it's been all right
working as Wardrobe Mistress and doing some dress-
making on the side . . . but sometimes, Win, just sometimes, I wonder what my life could have been if you and
Antoinette hadn't blocked my comeback . . .'

12

Danger! The sudden jolting awareness of imminent peril brought him wide awake a split-second before Tottie screamed.

Darkness! He started up, hitting his head on the shelf above him before he remembered where he was, who he was.

In that case, what had happened to his cat's-eye vision? He could not see a thing. Had he got locked inside the cabinet?

No . . . he pushed at the door and it gave easily, opening into further darkness. With increasing disquiet, he slid out into the room. It was completely dark . . . and silent.

Silent! Silent! That was the source of the danger: the life-support machine had stopped functioning.

'Power cut . . .' Tottie was half-sobbing. He heard her stumbling towards the door, towards the also completely dark corridor outside. 'Where's the emergency power? Nurse! Nurse! What's going on here? Why doesn't the stand-by generator kick in?'

Silence . . . Except, in the distance far below, he could hear what Tottie couldn't: the footsteps rushing about madly, the faint cries of panic, even a curse or two as what remained of the staff struggled to cope with the sudden emergency.

'Win! Oh God—Win!' Tottie fumbled her way back to the bed. 'Win, are you all right?' she called frantically. 'Where's your pulse? Oh God! I can't find it!'

No pulse? His fur bristled and rose. *No pulse?* What would happen to *him?* Would he be trapped for ever in Monty's body? No, not for ever—for the limited lifespan allotted to this small, furry, vulnerable body. A few more months . . . a few more years . . .

'Matches . . .' He heard Tottie muttering to herself. 'Matches . . . I picked up a booklet at that restaurant the other night.' He heard objects hitting the floor as she scrabbled through her handbag.

'Aaaah!' She had found them. There was the scrape of a match against the rough striking strip. A light flared.

'Win?' She bent over the recumbent form, lowering the flame towards his face. 'Win . . . ?'

The match went out.

'No! Oh no!' She struck another match, shielding it with her hand this time. As it neared his face, it went out again.

What was happening? He could no longer bear the suspense. He leaped for the pillow, disregarding the consequences.

He misjudged the leap. His claws sprang out automatically and dug deep, seeking to steady himself. They sank into soft vulnerable flesh.

'*Aaarrrgh!*' He recognized the voice as his own, strong and vibrant, pitched to reach the back of the gods. He retracted the claws quickly and, with Monty's reflexes, licked apologetically at the wounds.

'Win? Win?' Another match flared. He crouched low, trying to hide behind the raised, indignant shoulder.

'Win—say it again! Speak to Tottie!' She bent closer, the tiny flame wavering above The Instrument's nose and mouth. It flared up briefly, then vanished abruptly.

'DAD! DAD!' The shout resounded through the building. There was the thump of stairs being taken three at a time—and damn the danger of a broken leg—or neck. 'DAD!'

The electricity began an erratic humming . . . the lights flickered . . . the machines hiccoughed . . .

'DAD!' Geoffrey burst into the room. 'Dad—are you all right?'

They all saw the raised head, heard the indignant '*Gurrr . . .*' as the lights flickered one final time, then steadied into a constant glow.

The head sank back against the pillow, the eyes closed

. . . but the chest continued to heave with more vehemence than had been in evidence before.

'*Gurrr* . . .' came the last protest before Monty retreated back into silence and immobility.

'Oh, Geoff—' Tottie turned to greet Geoffrey and the cat took advantage of her distraction to leap to the floor and streak back into the shelter of the cabinet.

'Geoff, Geoff—' Tottie fell into his arms, laughing and sobbing. 'Win's going to be all right! He blew out the matches by himself. He doesn't need those awful machines any more. He can breathe without them!'

13

He felt safe with Geoffrey there watching over The Instrument. Good lad, Geoffrey. Another fighter. Right now he was giving Matron a well-deserved hard time.

'I want a full explanation of this.' Geoffrey's voice was cold enough to raise goose pimples on a polar bear.

'The power failed, you say. But there was no sign of power failure anywhere outside. The lights were on in houses along the way and the street lamps were all lit. It appears that the only power failure was within this building —a hospital! And what happened to your reserve supply? It was always my understanding that hospitals kept an emergency generator for such a situation.'

'We do, but—' Matron was flustered—and at bay. She was trying to hide something; he could hear it in her voice.

'But what?'

'We're investigating now. Something went wrong.'

'It certainly did!' Geoffrey was relentless. 'This is my father's life we're talking about. It's no thanks to St Monica's that he's still alive. If he'd been utterly dependent on that machine, he'd have been finished.'

That's right! If good old Monty hadn't kept the old bellows going, they'd have been booking the Memorial Service at St Paul's, Covent Garden, by the morning.

'Finished,' Geoffrey emphasized. 'Like that old boy across the hall.'

'Oh!' Matron took an involuntary step backwards.

'Did you think I didn't notice? It was pretty obvious when you just glanced in here, saw that my father was all right—and then disappeared. I could hear all the commotion across the hall—and then the silence.'

'I really cannot discuss the condition of other patients with you,' Matron said icily.

'You mean you don't dare. The patient is dead.'

'You can't—' Matron hesitated, obviously trying to choose which line to take—'be sure.'

'If he's still alive,' Geoffrey pointed out, 'then you've left him alone in a darkened room. With his life-support machine turned off.'

That was it! That was the source of the disquiet he still felt. There was no sound of the machine from the other room and, as Geoffrey had said, it was dark over there. The old boy had shuffled off this mortal coil when the power failed. *As he had been intended to do?*

Someone had tried to kill him at the theatre—had they followed him here to finish the job?

He felt again the blow to his back that had knocked him off the ladder and sent him crashing to the floor. *Jilly didn't think it was an accident.* She had procured pictures of his injury to prove it. A bitch, perhaps, but a clever bitch. That evidence would be invaluable when he was able to utilize it. Not if. When.

Mmm, Jilly . . . For an instant, he recalled the calculating note in her voice when she spoke of how much better her exclusive story would be if Winstanley Fortescue were to die . . . And the photographer had wistfully remarked that the 'last pictures' would fetch a far higher price . . .

No! No! That was paranoid! That was no reason to kill a man. Besides, Jilly had not been at the theatre when the first attempt was made. No, someone had to have a more personal reason. But what?

'And speaking of those infernal machines—' Geoffrey continued to give no quarter—'it's time you disconnected my father. He's proved he doesn't need it; he can manage on his own.'

'You'll have to speak to Doctor about that.' Matron fell back with relief on a Higher Authority. 'I can't do anything like that without his permission. He'll be doing his rounds in the morning, about ten. You can talk to him then.'

'Oh yes?' Geoffrey came close to sneering. 'And what if something else happens before then? You've had a power failure, suppose there's a power surge? The machine could actively harm him then.'

'That isn't likely—'

'Neither was a power failure, so you tell me.'

'We have precautions built into the machine against such an eventuality.'

'The same way you had an emergency generator ready to take over?'

Good lad! The boy really cared about his dad; he wasn't going to let these medical morons get away with a thing. Keep fighting, boyo! Oh, I'm really getting to know you now. We'll have some great times together . . . when all this is over.

'There was a loose connection—' In her apologetic confusion, Matron let too much slip. 'It's been fixed now.'

'In good time for your next power failure?'

'Our power didn't fail! The master switch in the fuse box slipped—' She stopped abruptly.

Slipped—or was thrown? So that was how it had been done. Murder by remote control. A coward's way. The method of someone who wanted to do the vile deed without seeing the effect it had, without watching the victim die.

So, a coward—and an opportunist. Someone who saw the chance and acted on impulse. Also someone who was criminally stupid—a killer who had killed the wrong victim . . .

Absently, he licked a paw and dabbed at his face with it; strange, how soothing it was to wash himself like this. Also, it seemed to help his concentration. There was a lot to think about; no wonder cats were so clean.

'You'll have to speak with Doctor in the morning.' The voice rose as high as a professionally soothing voice could decently rise in exceptional circumstances. The heels clicked across the floor with a sound of finality. The subject was closed.

'Don't worry, Dad.' There was the scrape of a chair being pulled up beside the bed. 'We'll get to the bottom of this. I'll stay right here until morning and nab the doctor as soon as he arrives.

'In fact—' the chair scraped away again—'I'd better go down and telephone Cynthia. She was going to take the next shift. I'll tell her I'm staying the night and she can come in at eight a.m.'

She won't like that. Cynthia was not a morning person— one reason why she hadn't got farther in the film industry . . . in the days when there was a film industry. The theatre suited her better; matinees were the earliest occasions for which she was prepared to rise and shine.

Geoffrey had left the room—temporarily. Cautiously, he poked his nose out and looked around. Emptiness and silence . . . good! He crossed the floor to the side of the bed, gathered himself together and sprang—landing, as he had intended, on the pillow.

Something quivered in the still face beside him, but the eyes remained obstinately shut. Well, what had he expected?

Monty . . . Monty, old boy. He nuzzled at an ear, a soft mewling sound broke from him. *Can you hear me? Can you understand? What are we going to do?*

An answering muffled sound growled low in The Instrument's throat; its eyes opened and looked around wildly. It recognized itself, but didn't know what to do about it. Well, neither did he.

Take it easy . . . Was he getting through, or were they still two different species, as far apart as ever?

The head moved, trying to meet his head and rub against it.

*By George—there was a thought.*That was the way it had happened—was it the way out?

There was a bruise on The Instrument's forehead, in roughly about the same spot where his own forehead ached. He aimed himself at it and bumped against it. Nothing happened. But Monty did not flinch away; he seemed to know what was being tried.

He aimed at the bruise again and hit it harder. Something flickered deep inside his skull. Again! He backed off and hurled himself at the bruise. Monty whimpered at the pain and the machinery by the bedside flickered and changed tone.

He backed to the foot of the bed and prepared to charge forward in a fresh assault—

'I see you!' The voice from the doorway halted him before he could start. He crouched low, hoping she hadn't been addressing him.

'What are you doing in here, cat? I'm sure you shouldn't be here.' Dame Theodora advanced into the room, frowning through her spectacles.

'And Win!' She stopped by the bedside and looked down at its famous occupant.

'So the little toad wasn't lying! Oliver brought me my glasses and—' She did not appear to notice that she was getting no response from her old friend.

'He told me you were here—but I didn't really believe him. What's the matter with *you*?' She laughed abruptly. 'What's a nice man like you doing in a place like this?'

Monty lay motionless, watching warily as she bent over him. But hers was a familiar voice, a known form; he was not alarmed. His head rose slightly in greeting.

The cat crept forward, impelled by instincts beyond Win's control. *Nice lady. Friend. Food,* something deep within his temporary form kept insisting. He remembered that Dame Theodora's last two shows had been staged at the Chesterton. Of course, Monty knew her.

'And you.' She noticed the cat was advancing slowly, as though against its better judgement. 'How did you get in here?' She frowned again and adjusted her glasses.

'Wait a minute—I know you! You're Monty! You're the Chesterton cat. What are *you* doing here?'

Vaguely alarmed, the cat hesitated and crouched again. Dame Theodora, something inside him insisted, inclined to the capricious—much given to suddenly flapping her hand and driving him away just when he was settling down for an evening in her lap. What sort of a mood was she in tonight?

'Monty—' She stretched out her hand invitingly. 'Dear old Monty. Come on, Monty, you know me. Come to Theodora,' she crooned. 'There's a good boy. Good Monty, come here . . . come . . .'

In horror, he saw The Instrument lurch upwards in response to the call and begin to roll off the bed, aiming itself in Theodora's direction.

The wavy lines on the monitoring panels broke into mountain peaks and tunnel troughs; electronic bleeps went into hysterical overdrive. Lights flashed, warning bells rang.

With a gasp of consternation, Dame Theodora stepped backwards, turned and ran from the room, all hell breaking loose behind her.

He paused only long enough to wince in sympathy as The Instrument, unfamiliar limbs flailing awkwardly, landed on the floor and sprawled there, winded.

Then he turned and raced from the room, following Theodora to the staircase.

Below, he could hear the uproar as what remained of the staff rallied to face the new emergency. The elevator whined, voices rose in hubbub.

Once again, feet took the stairs three at a time, as Geoffrey bellowed: 'DAD! . . . DAD! . . .'

14

'Auntie Thea, where have you been?' Oliver Crump was in the sitting-room, scribbling in a spiral notebook. He rose and moved forward as his aunt entered her suite.

'What are you doing here?' Dame Theodora asked ungraciously. 'I thought you were at the theatre slandering someone's talent tonight.'

'The show ended an hour ago. I thought I'd just look in on you before dropping my review off at the office.'

'Is that what you're doing with that notebook? Stop it immediately! I will not have you perpetrating your obscenities in my suite.'

'Just a few notes, Auntie Thea.' He disposed of the notebook hastily, his voice placating. 'How are you? I've been worried about you. The place was dark when I got here. I couldn't see a thing and I couldn't find anyone to ask about it. Fortunately, the power came on again just in time for me to use the lift—'

'You ought to use the stairs. Work some of the flab off you!'

'Then, when you weren't here—' Crump was an expert at not hearing anything he didn't want to hear; that—and his rhinoceros hide—had taken him to his present position —'I sat down to wait for you. I hoped you hadn't gone too far.'

'Hoped I hadn't got away, you mean.' Dame Theodora stalked past him and sat in the armchair opposite, patting her lap in invitation to Monty.

'Where did you get that cat?' Oliver frowned. 'Surely they don't allow animals in a hospital? Have you been outside?'

'Mind your own business!' She patted her lap again and the cat leaped into it. They both sat there glaring at Oliver.

'And you can keep your mouth shut about the cat. He's better company than you are.'

'I can see you're in one of your moods.' Oliver gave a put-upon sigh. 'Did you eat any dinner? You know you've got to keep your strength up.'

'The food is disgusting!' Dame Theodora swept her hand towards the congealing creamed chicken. A low moan escaped from the cat and he gazed ravenously at the abandoned meal.

'Do you want it, Monty?' She looked down at him. 'I suppose it can't hurt you. Your guts are constructed to cope with anything, aren't they? Even this sort of muck.' She set the dish down on the floor; the cat leaped from her lap and dived for it.

'I don't approve.' Oliver shook his head, knowing how little his approval would mean to his aunt. 'Germs—'

'You're the only germ around here!' She watched him bow his head in exaggerated patience. 'A germ—and a worm. I'm glad your mother isn't alive today to see the depths you've sunk to.'

'Please, Auntie Thea.'

'And what did you think of the play tonight?' She changed tack abruptly. 'Whose throats are you cutting for the amusement of your moronic readers tomorrow?'

'I guess it's time to leave—'

'I asked you a question!' Even the cat joined her in an accusing glare.

'It wasn't a very good play. Honestly it wasn't, Auntie Thea.' His hangdog look endeared him neither to aunt nor feline. 'And the actors were . . . miscast, to put it at its most charitable.'

'Since when were *you* ever charitable?'

'I'll have a copy of the paper delivered to you.' Oliver began backing towards the door. 'You can read it for yourself—'

'Hello! I thought I heard familiar voices.' Jilly blocked the doorway, her greedy, gleaning eyes taking in the scene.

'Oliver, darling, what are you doing here? Oh, I see—' She looked at Dame Theodora. 'This is a personal visit, then, not professional?'

'Oliver—?' Dame Theodora's voice rose dangerously. 'Who is this . . . creature?'

'Sorry, Auntie Thea, I didn't realize you hadn't met. This is Jilly Zanna. She works on the *London Record*. Does a lot of celebrity interviews. I'm surprised you two haven't—'

'Monty!' Dame Theodora stooped and swept the cat into her arms. (Luckily he had finished everything on the plate.) 'Monty, we are surrounded by reptiles!'

How true, how true. And how clever of dear old Thea to cut to the crux of the matter. But he could not resist a yawn. The feeling slid over him that he could deal with this situation better after he'd had a little nap. A catnap, *heh-heh-heh.*

'Where did that cat come from?' Jilly stared at the sharp pointed teeth on full display and the pink curling tongue. 'How did he get inside again?'

'Reptiles,' Dame Theodora crooned to the cat. 'Ugly, nasty . . . and dangerous. Have nothing to do with them, Monty.'

'I'm afraid she's not at her best tonight,' Oliver apologized. 'But what are you doing here?'

'I . . .' Jilly lowered her eyelids, improbably demure. 'I came to see Win. He's here, you know.'

'He's downstairs.' Oliver looked at her sharply. 'What are you doing up on this floor?'

'Spying, I expect,' Dame Theodora said. 'I've heard about you and Win. Has Miranda found out yet?'

'Auntie Thea, please—'

'I had a friend with me,' Jilly said quickly. 'We got separated when the lights went out. I've been looking for him.'

'What's the matter with Win?' Dame Theodora

demanded. 'Why are the vultures gathering? Why is he wired up to those machines? Was it a heart attack?'

'No, he had an accident at rehearsal. Took a nasty fall.' Oliver's eyes suddenly narrowed. 'How do you know he's wired up to machines? Have you been snooping, Auntie Thea?'

'The nurse told me.' The flat statement defied him to call her a liar.

'And why are *you* here, Dame Theodora?' Jilly cooed. 'Nothing serious, I hope? You look quite well. Not a spot of your old trouble, is it?'

'You suggest one word of that in print and we'll sue!' Oliver snapped. 'Auntie Thea is simply here for a rest before she begins her new film in a couple of weeks.'

'Of course,' Jilly said. 'I quite understand. Some people find it quite easy to rest at home, but Dame Theodora is obviously one of those who find that there are too many . . . distractions . . . available.'

'One word . . .' Oliver warned. 'You can't afford another libel suit, Jilly. You know the Lords and Masters are beginning to reckon you're too expensive to maintain.'

'Maybe.' Jilly's eyes gleamed. 'But if the stories are good enough, I can write my own ticket to a better paper. Perhaps even a television show.'

So that was it! That was why she had always been so anxious to accompany him to the TV studio when he was working on the pilot for that proposed Anglo-American series about a pair of rival management executives in the same international company who had both been made redundant and, unable to find new employment at their ages in a recessionary market, had joined forces to become confidence tricksters and take revenge on the company that had cast them out. The project had gone into abeyance, in the mysterious way that television projects were prone to do and only time would tell whether it had slipped into a black hole or would become activated again at some future —and probably highly inconvenient—date.

Now, for instance. What more inconvenient time could there be? He gave a shudder as he pictured The Instrument —precariously controlled by Monty—trying to go through its paces in front of the cameras.

'Be careful, Jilly.' Suddenly, Oliver Crump looked sinister. 'Be very careful.'

'Why, Oliver—' Jilly's laugh was uncertain—'you sound as though you're threatening me.'

'Do I?' Oliver's smile was dangerous. 'What a pity you haven't any witnesses. My aunt didn't hear a thing. And the cat won't talk.'

Don't be too sure of that. The cat glared impartially from Jilly to Oliver.

'So it's like that, is it?' Jilly allowed her open hostility to show. 'Try being careful yourself, Oliver. Better men than you have thought they could tell me what to do. They found out . . .'

'Aaaah-ooh.' Dame Theodora yawned widely.

'We're tiring you, Auntie Thea.' Oliver was well-trained to take a hint. 'It's late. Go to bed and get a good night's sleep. I'll come to visit you again tomorrow.'

'Don't bother,' she said, yawning again.

The cat yawned in sympathy. Sleep . . . it sounded so-o-o good. He blinked slowly, trying to fight the creeping laziness that told him to relax, curl up beside Thea on the bed and sleep . . .

He felt himself being gathered up and carried towards the bedroom.

'Perhaps I might drop in and see you again tomorrow, Dame Theodora.' Jilly was still in there trying. 'We could do an interview. It would be good advance publicity for your film.'

'Perhaps.' Dame Theodora turned and looked at her, accurately gauging the nuisance value her next remark would have for her nephew. 'Make sure you bring a bottle of gin with you, if you do.'

'You didn't hear that, Jilly.' Oliver caught her arm so

tightly that she gasped in pain. 'And you'll do no such thing!'

'You will, if you want an interview.'

'Auntie Thea, you keep out of this!'

'And you mind your manners, Oliver!' She loosened her grip on the cat and it slid to the floor and retreated to a corner, watching the combatants.

Why Oliver was fighting a losing battle to protect Dame Theodora's reputation, he didn't know. Everyone in the theatre, and most of those outside it, had understood for years the reason for her periodic withdrawals from society. In fact, if she would only withdraw to the Betty Ford Clinic in a blaze of publicity, it would probably give fresh impetus to her career. A good spicy interview with Jilly might have the same effect.

'Let go of me!' Jilly's temper was rising. 'I'll have bruises.'

'You'll be lucky if that's all—' Oliver wrestled Jilly with one hand and the doorknob with the other. The door swung open abruptly.

'Jilly!' The photographer was just outside. 'I've been looking for you. Is this where you've been?'

'Where have *you* been?' Jilly glared at him, then narrowed her eyes and slanted her gaze meaningly from his camera to Dame Theodora.

'Up on the roof.' Casually, Jake moved his camera up into position. 'Got a few great shots of London at night.'

'Will you all get out of here!' Oliver snapped.

'Sure, guv. Just a minute—' The camera flashed, then again.

'Stop that!' Oliver released his hold on Jilly to follow the photographer as he danced around Dame Theodora snapping off several shots.

Thea obligingly changed pose and expression as he circled her.

'Dear boy,' she cooed. 'I'm not dressed properly for this.'

'You look great,' he assured her. 'Just turn this way a bit more—'

'Stop it!' Oliver's voice rose to a shriek. 'That does it!' He stabbed at the button to summon an attendant. 'I'm having you thrown out!'

'Don't bother.' Jilly headed for the door. 'Come on, Jake, we're leaving.'

'You certainly are! And furthermore, I'm seeing to it that you're barred from the premises,' Oliver announced. 'I'll make sure they never let you in here again!'

'Oh?' Jilly looked at him coldly, then flung her defiance into the room behind him.

'Gordon's or Beefeater's?' she called.

15

Miranda, exhausted, slept until nearly noon. As soon as she plugged the telephone in, it began ringing. For a moment, her spirit quailed, then she remembered.

Win was better, a lot better. It was safe to answer the telephone again.

'Hello . . . ?' She caught up the receiver and spoke eagerly.

'Oh . . .' Some of her enthusiasm dwindled. 'Rufus, hello. I didn't expect to hear from you so early. Only . . . it isn't *that* early, is it? . . . No, no, I haven't seen the papers yet.' Her voice grew cold. 'And I never read the *London Record*.'

There was a staccato burst of words from the other end of the line, like a machine-gun, mowing down everything in its path. She listened incredulously.

'They said *what*?' Yet why was she so shocked and indignant? She had had the same thought herself. But she had been overwrought then, her nerves frayed, her endurance close to its limits. She had fought herself back from that crisis of confidence, that abyss of suspicion, back to a sane and rational world where such things could never happen. Why should anyone want to kill Win? What had he done to offend that much?

'Picture? They've printed pictures?' The world spun out of alignment again. *Proof?* How could there be proof of something so unthinkable?

'Is something wrong, dear?' Tottie stood in the doorway, watching her with concern. How long had she been standing there?

'No.' The answer was automatic, prompted by a rush of irritation. She had forgotten that Tottie had stayed the night—or what was left of it—again. It had seemed sensible at the time. Tottie had come to report what had happened during the power cut at St Monica's. It would have been heartless to send her back to her little flat in the suburbs —even in a minicab—at that hour. Especially when there was a guest room available and Tottie knew it; had, in fact, dropped a hopeful little hint about it. It would have been churlish to send her out into the night; after all, it had been her vigil at Win's bedside that had meant her missing the last train home.

'Oh.' Tottie advanced into the room. 'I thought you sounded upset. I was afraid—'

'I mean, yes.' Miranda corrected herself. 'But not "wrong" the way you meant it . . . What? No, sorry, Rufus, I wasn't talking to you. Tottie just asked me something. Yes, she's here. No, no, it isn't necessary for you to come over—' Miranda felt herself growing distracted. Everyone meant so well, but never seemed to realize that a person needed some time alone to try to assimilate what was happening. The right to privacy was the first thing lost in a crisis. Others felt it their duty to crowd in on one and seize responsibility for the ordinary minutiæ of life on the grounds that they were 'helping'.

'Yes, of course, you'll be welcome. But—Rufus? Rufus?' She replaced the phone with a sigh. Sometimes such interference—er, help—was welcome. At other times . . .

'Tottie,' she said impulsively. 'Could you be an angel and run out and get the newspapers? Especially—' she tried not to choke—'the *London Record*.'

'Oh dear.' Tottie understood instantly. 'They've got the story about the accident, have they? Well, I suppose we couldn't keep it under wraps for ever.'

'It's worse than that.' Suddenly, Tottie was a beloved friend and ally again. 'Much, much worse. That's why Rufus was calling. Just get the papers and you'll see.'

With Tottie out of the house, she felt as though her home was her own again, however briefly.

Very briefly. The telephone rang again. When she picked it up, the voice was unmistakably that of a journalist-on-the-make.

'What can you tell me about the murder attempt on Winstanley Fortescue?' it began without preamble—probably knowing the shrift any preamble would get and hoping to take the answerer by surprise. 'Who were his enemies? Who do you suspect?'

'Sorry, you have a wrong number.' She yanked the plug out of its connection and replaced the dead phone.

Dead. She discovered that the wild panic had not left her, it had just lain dormant while she slept. Slept for long hours, when anything might have happened. *Win!* She dropped to her knees and scrabbled to plug in the telephone again.

It began ringing immediately. No, not the hospital—another bloody journalist! How they fed off each other, discovering their stories in others' papers. She disconnected without speaking and began dialling rapidly before any more of them could get through.

After the obligatory delay, St Monica's grudgingly saw that Geoffrey received the call. He sounded fraught and exhausted—but cheerful.

'Dad's not bad, not bad, at all. Pretty good, in fact, considering that he fell out of bed—'

'Fell out of bed?' Miranda heard herself shriek. 'How did that happen?'

'We're not quite sure. No one was around at the time. I was—' Geoffrey defended himself from a charge of negligence she had not made—'I was downstairs telephoning Cynthia when all hell suddenly broke loose. They tried to persuade me to stay there, but I could tell from the way they were looking at me that it was something to do with Dad.

'I ran upstairs. They were furious—but they couldn't stop me. They knew I knew. They knew I'd make trouble if—' He broke off and she could hear him swallow.

'I ran into his room—and there he was. On the floor beside the bed—on his hands and knees—half the wires and tubes still hanging from him. He saw me and started crawling towards me—on all fours. Oh, Miranda—' For a moment, his youth showed through. 'Miranda, it was awful! I thought—

'But he was all right, just a few more bruises. Then they put him back into bed and connected him up again. I tried to stop them. I keep telling them he doesn't need those machines any more. In fact, they seem to worry him. He can make it on his own now. He just needs to be left alone to have time to recover peacefully. Without doctors pulling and prying at him—'

'I agree!' Miranda felt a resolution form and harden. But it wasn't just the doctors and medical staff—

'Have you seen the newspapers this morning?'

'What?' Her sudden change of subject bewildered him. 'No. Why? Should I have? Why?'

'Jilly—' Miranda's voice chilled. 'His *friend*, Jilly—'

'Has—?' Geoffrey swallowed audibly again. 'She hasn't got the story . . . has she?'

'Rufus just rang me. Tottie's gone to get the papers now. Rufus says there are photographs . . . of Win in bed . . . in St Monica's.'

'Photographs?' Geoffrey's voice rose unbelievingly. 'Of

Dad? Here? How did she find out? How did she get in?'

'My questions exactly,' Miranda said. 'Also *when* did she get in? Was she the reason Win fell out of bed? If they were trying to take photographs—'

'She must have sneaked in when the lights went off. Perhaps she was the one who turned them off. Otherwise, someone was with Dad every minute.' Sudden guilt tinged his voice. 'Except for the few minutes I went downstairs to telephone.'

Miranda heard the front door slam. Tottie's footsteps, hurrying down the hall, were nearly as loud as her lamentations.

'Oh, oh, oh dear . . .' She came into the room, the *London Record* unfolded before her. 'Win won't like this. He won't like it at all. He'll be furious.'

'Hold on, Geoffrey, Tottie's just come back.'

'Look! Just look!' Tottie waved the newspaper under her appalled eyes. 'Right across a double-page spread—bare as the day he was born!'

'Oh my God! Win will kill someone for this!' Miranda found her heart leaped up. This was the end of Jilly.

'Do you think there's any truth in it?' Tottie asked, almost timidly, indicating the headline:

'OR WAS HE PUSHED?' The sinister black bruise on the small of Win's back had been thoughtfully arrowed so that the most illiterate of the mental defectives who composed the alleged readership of Jilly's rag could not miss it.

'Miranda—?' Geoffrey said. 'Miranda, are you still there?'

'He shouldn't have a bruise in that spot,' Tottie said. 'He fell head first. We all saw him. He smashed into poor Monty head to head. They're both probably still confused.' She looked around vaguely. 'Where *is* poor Monty? I haven't seen him since yesterday. You don't think he got worse and crawled away into a corner to die? That's what cats do, you know. They go off by themselves and—'

'Miranda—?' Geoffrey called anxiously.

Miranda stared at the bruise with growing horror. *Had* someone actually tried to kill Win?

Worse, were they still trying? That increasingly suspicious power failure meant that the life-support system had stopped. If Win hadn't been strong enough to continue breathing . . .

And what had happened just before Geoffrey had returned to the room to find him on his hands and knees on the floor?

'Miranda—?'

'I'm coming right over, Geoffrey,' she said. 'I'm signing Win out of that place. I'm bringing him home where we can watch over him.'

16

It wasn't quite that easy.

'I'm not sure this is wise, Miranda.' Rufus had arrived just in time to accompany them to the hospital. 'The best medical science can offer is right at Win's bedside at St Monica's. If you bring him home and any problems develop—' He glanced sideways at her to see how she was taking his advice. 'You know you'd never forgive yourself if anything happened.'

'And where was medical science when the lights went out?' Tottie weighed in on Miranda's side. 'I thought I'd die when I realized the machines had stopped working. And I was sure Win was a goner.'

'Yes, but that sort of accident couldn't happen again in a hundred years.' Rufus let his irritation with Tottie show in his voice. 'Do you realize the odds against it?'

'About the same as the odds for Win being found on the hospital floor shortly afterwards, I'd say.' Miranda's voice was cold. 'What *are* the odds against three serious "accidents" happening to the same person within forty-eight hours, Rufus? You're the gambler. You ought to know.'

'Things like that happen once in a while,' Rufus admitted. 'We call it a losing streak. Remember when you were in three flops in a row?'

'I *told* you *The Dream Beyond the Moon* would never run.' It had been a mistake to remind Miranda of that. It did not reinforce her confidence in his judgement.

'Ooooo, yes.' Tottie winced. 'That poetry and moonshine lark is always very tricky. You may draw your cult audience, but they can't keep a show running for very long. And the way that poor author committed suicide after you got his hopes up and then closed the show didn't go down well, either.'

'All right! All right!' Rufus snarled. 'That's water under the bridge and not the subject under discussion. We're talking about Win—and what's best for him.'

'Of course, that show might have run a while longer if Win hadn't pulled out so suddenly, the way he did.' Tottie was still caught up in the past. 'It was too—'

'Here we are!' Miranda clawed at the door as the taxi swept up the drive and pulled to a halt at the entrance to St Monica's. Nothing happened. Damn these new taxis and their driver-controlled locks! The stupid sod wasn't going to release the lock until he'd had his money. Did they look as though—?

'Right! Good!' Rufus brandished his wallet and, reassured by the sight, the driver released the mechanism. Miranda half-tumbled out and fought to regain her balance. Tottie was right behind her and put out a hand to steady her.

'You go ahead.' Rufus waved them onward. 'I'll catch you up.' He turned and went into consultation with the driver.

'We'll see you upstairs,' Tottie said, following Miranda as she plunged through the entrance without a backward glance.

'That's right, dear, you go ahead.' Panting, Tottie echoed Rufus's words. 'I'm right behind you.' She sighed as Miranda ignored the lift and raced up the staircase. 'Right behind . . .'

Traffic jam! Miranda paused in the doorway and looked around. Geoffrey was leaning towards Cynthia in what could only be called a placatory way. Peter Farley hovered just inside the door, looking apologetic but determined. Win lay silently on the bed, one eye closed, the other eye half open. Typical! Taking in everything that was going on, but remaining uninvolved.

'Afraid we've got our wires crossed,' Peter Farley was saying. 'Last I heard, this was *my* tour of duty.'

'Sorry, old man,' Geoffrey said. 'I stayed the night—and then some. I put Cynthia off a couple of times, but I forgot you were next on the list.'

'I'll leave you to it, then,' Cynthia said with relief. 'I'm exhausted. One telephone call after another all night! Geoffrey kept changing his mind about what he was doing. This has all been—'

'Good morning,' Miranda said crisply. 'All present and accounted for, I see.'

'Miranda.' Cynthia greeted her without enthusiasm. 'How *are* you? *You* got some rest, I hope?'

'A little, yes. Hello, Win.' Strangely, she felt awkward about bestowing even the chastest peck in front of all the watching eyes. She settled for resting her hand gently on his cheek and knew that she had done the right thing when he nestled gratefully into it.

'Don't worry, darling,' she said. 'You're coming home.'

'Actually—' Geoffrey looked worried—'I mentioned that idea to the doctor. He's rather against it. He suggests you wait until Sir Reginald has had a chance to examine him. If Sir Reginald agrees, then he'll agree. Until then, he thinks you ought to postpone the decision.'

'It's not a bad idea, Miranda.' Rufus had joined them.

He nodded to the others in the company before continuing.
'A second professional opinion, that's the ticket. Reggie's
flight should be getting in just about now. Give him some
time to clear Customs and Immigration; he's coming
straight to St Monica's. He'll check Win over and let you
know what he thinks. I wouldn't be surprised if you got your
own way. If you ask me, Win looks a lot better already.' He
raised his voice cheerily. 'You're doing fine, aren't you, old
boy?'

Win closed his eye and seemed to withdraw. Miranda
took it as a hopeful sign. Rufus often had that effect on him.

'At least, I got them to take most of the tubes out,' Geoffrey said. 'They were going to do him more harm than good
if he began moving around and trying to get out of bed.'
Geoffrey closed his eyes against an uncomfortable memory.
'Some of them had come out anyway when he fell.'

'Ummm, yes . . .' Rufus began losing colour. He was
not, Miranda remembered, very good about accidents or
emergencies. He was the first to demand the attendance of
the St John's Ambulance Brigade, even though a situation
called for nothing more professional than the Stage Manager wielding a bottle of smelling salts.

'Well, . . .' Rufus looked as though he could use some
smelling salts himself now. 'Who's minding the theatre?
We're holding a rehearsal after lunch. Is anyone planning
to attend?'

'Yes, yes, of course,' Peter Farley said guiltily. He knew
for whom the rehearsal was being called. 'I was just going
to sit with Win for a couple of hours first. I thought it
was my turn, but they forgot to tell me about the changed
arrangements. I was planning to read over my part aloud.
I thought, perhaps, the words might get through to him
and help pull him out of the coma.'

'That's true,' Tottie said. 'If Win thought someone else
was stepping into his part, it would be enough to raise
him up from the dead. Oooops!' She glanced nervously at
Miranda. 'Sorry, dear.'

Miranda made a forgiving dismissive gesture. Tact-lessness was the least of their problems right now.

'Oh! I didn't know there was a *party* going on!' Another problem—Antoinette—stood in the doorway, Jennet immediately behind her.

Rufus groaned and muttered something inaudible and probably obscene under his breath.

'Antoinette.' Miranda controlled herself with an effort. 'And Jennet.' She managed a genuine smile for the young girl; her mother wasn't her fault. It was Win who should have had better taste.

'Hello, Mother, Jen.' Geoffrey looked awkward, as well he might. He had obviously told Antoinette that this would be a good time for her to slip in and see Win without anyone else knowing. It was typical of Antoinette's paranoia that she should imagine that anyone—that Miranda—would be upset by her appearance.

'Geoffrey told me what you were doing.' Antoinette had always believed that attack was the best defence; no wonder poor Win had found it increasingly difficult to live with her. 'About setting up a roster of old friends and colleagues to come and sit with Win and reminisce about old times. I can't understand why you didn't start with me. After all, Win and I have shared more years and memories together than anyone else here.'

Including you dangled unsaid at the end of that sentence.

'It's early days yet, dear,' Tottie rushed in placatingly. 'Don't worry, we'll all have our turn.'

'Actually, that may not be necessary now,' Miranda said quickly. 'Win seems to have come out of the coma.'

'Not that it seems to be doing him much good.' Tottie looked critically at the closed eyes and shuttered face. 'He's still not really with us. Not properly.'

'Sir Reginald will be here soon,' Miranda said. 'We'll have a better idea of the situation after he's done his tests.'

'I don't know what I'm doing here at all,' Cynthia complained. 'I had understood I was supposed to sit here alone with Win and talk to him and try to draw him back to life. I even—' Her voice rose querulously; the Ministering Angel upstaged by the rest of the heavenly host. 'I even brought a book of poetry along to read to him. And I get here—and find a Crowd Scene!'

She had a point there, Miranda had to admit. The room was too full of well-wishers. (Or was it? Were they all *well-wishers*?) Too many people, anyway.

'I'm not terribly sorry.' Geoffrey was beginning to sound harassed. 'I should have kept better track of everything, but we had problems here and I got distracted. All the arrangement just went out of my head.'

'I hope the lines of your part don't.' Cynthia was sliding into a nasty mood.

'Geoffrey will be brilliant!' Antoinette rushed to her son's defence. 'If the rest of the cast are half as good—' She glared from Cynthia to Peter—'no one will miss Win at all.'

'Oh dear,' Tottie mourned. 'The party's getting rough.'

'Mother, you don't mean that,' Geoffrey said. Jennet withdrew quietly from her mother's side and slipped across the room to the window where she stood looking down at the lawn below.

'Yes, she does,' Cynthia said. 'She never really gave a damn for Win. Never!'

'I suppose that's the excuse you gave yourself for rushing in to take him away from me!' Antoinette's voice rose.

'You never had him to be taken away from you!' Cynthia snarled.

The noise level in the room was rising alarmingly. Miranda considered intervening, then decided to stay out of it. Anything she said was likely to result in both sides turning against her.

'Now let's be calm—' Rufus tried, on the theory that the hand that signed the paychecks was the least likely to get bitten in the fray.

'Perhaps I ought to get back to the theatre.' Peter Farley

started for the door, but stopped just short of the doorway.

'Dame Theodora!' He stood aside to allow her to enter.

'You're making enough noise down here to wake the dead!' She swept in, Monty cradled in her arms and looked around disdainfully.

'Why is Win that peculiar colour? And why is he twitching like that?'

17

Any cat would twitch, surrounded by ex-mistresses, so to speak, and with all that noise going on. The furry body wriggled uncomfortably in Dame Theodora's arms. She tightened her hold on him; he was her prop in this scene and he wasn't going to get away.

'Win!' Hostilities ceased abruptly as Miranda rushed over to the figure on the bed. 'Win!' She took his hand and felt it respond faintly. Or was it just another twitch?

'Where's the nurse?' she cried frantically. 'The doctor?'

In the background, someone pushed a call button.

'His colour is a little better now.' Dame Theodora stalked over to the bed and gazed down judiciously. 'Not twitching so much, either. The man needs some peace and quiet, if you ask me.'

The cat in her arms gave a short assenting yowl. The figure on the bed risked opening one eye to try to pinpoint the sound.

'Win!' The eye closed again as Miranda bent over him, blocking his view. 'Win—speak to me, darling!'

'*Mirreeow!*' It was torn from him. He struggled to reach her, but Dame Theodora held tight.

'Monty!' Tottie started forward. 'It *is* Monty! What are you doing here?'

'What are *all* these people doing here?' Dame Theodora

countered, keeping her grip on Monty as Tottie reached out to take him.

'That's right.' Miranda straightened and frowned at the assembly. 'How did you all get in, anyway? What are they thinking about on the Reception Desk to allow everyone to crowd in on a sick man like this?'

'There wasn't anyone there when I came in,' Peter Farley said defensively.

'They're understaffed at the moment.' Geoffrey spoke at the same time. 'The 'flu epidemic has hit them hard.'

'Lax!' Dame Theodora pronounced severely. 'Scandalously lax! The place is going downhill rapidly. They even keep letting my nephew in.'

The figure on the bed twitched again.

'That's enough!' Miranda's patience snapped, her temper flared. 'Out! All of you! Out of here!'

'That's right,' Tottie seconded her. 'There are too many of you. It's upsetting Win.'

'His children have a right to be here!' Antoinette prepared to stand her ground. 'And so do I!'

'You can come back later.' Tottie tried to reason with her. 'One at a time.'

'I was just leaving,' Peter Farley said truthfully—and thankfully. 'Ooops!' Again, he nearly collided with someone in the doorway.

'Clear this room!' The sharp voice of command, reinforced by Matron's crisp uniform, allowed no further argument. 'Immediately!'

Peter completed his exit. Jennet, avoiding her mother's eyes, was right behind him.

'I've been here all night.' Geoffrey seemed to feel that he ought to apologize to Miranda. 'I *would* like to get a bit of rest before rehearsal . . .'

'Use the chaise-longue in my dressing-room,' she said. '*Our* dressing-room.'

'Rest?' Cynthia's tone made it clear that *she* had been deprived not only of sleep, but of pleasant dreams and peace

of mind. 'Rest?' She gave a short bitter laugh for empha-
sis. 'At a time like this? When poor darling Win—' She
stretched out her arms towards him yearningly.

Miranda stepped in front of him. 'It's time to go now,
Cynthia,' she said firmly. 'I'll ring you later.'

'You won't need to ring *me* later,' Antoinette said.
'Because I'm not going.'

'Rufus—?' Miranda appealed over her head.

'Yes.' Sighing, he moved forward and put an arm around
Antoinette's shoulders. 'Let's go and have lunch. Anywhere
you like.'

'Well . . .' Antoinette allowed herself to be bribed, but
flashed a dangerous look at Miranda, warning that she'd
be back. Miranda hadn't doubted it.

Win had begun breathing more easily as the room
cleared. His eyes remained obstinately closed, but she knew
that he was conscious.

'That goes for the rest of you, too!' Matron crossed to
Win and automatically reached for his pulse. 'Out!'

'I'm his wife,' Miranda said coldly. 'I'm waiting for his
personal physician to arrive. Sir Reginald is flying in from
the States and should be here at any moment.'

'Go ahead, throw me out!' Dame Theodora challenged.
'I'd love to get out of this hell-hole. Unfortunately, I have
the misfortune to be in residence here.'

'We'll take you back to your room in a minute, Dame
Theodora.' Matron's eyes narrowed as she looked at Dame
Theodora for the first time. 'Where did you get that cat?'

'He dropped in to visit me. We're old friends, aren't we,
Monty?'

'The cat goes! Now!' Matron's attention was distracted
as the patient moved abruptly. She looked down at him,
frowning.

'I'll take Monty back to the theatre with me.' Tottie
started forward. 'That's where he belongs, isn't it, Monty?
Come on, Monty. Come to Tottie—'

The figure on the bed opened its eyes and looked around

wildly. It began to struggle, trying to free its wrist from Matron's grip.

'Please leave! The patient is becoming agitated.' Matron shifted her grip and tried to hold him down. 'Can't you see—?'

Easy, Monty, easy . . . The cat broke free and leaped on to the bed, uttering sounds that were half-purrs, half-cries.

'That's better,' Matron said as the patient stopped struggling. She swept one hand at the cat, trying to brush him off the bed.

He dodged her easily and moved up so that cat and man were face to face with each other, looking into each other's eyes.

In slow motion, both leaned forward so that their foreheads were touching. Slowly they rocked their heads from side to side, rubbing foreheads, eyes closed. The cat's purr could be heard throughout the room; the man uttered strange little sounds of contentment.

'Look at that,' Tottie said wonderingly. 'I never knew Win and Monty were so fond of each other. Isn't that sweet?'

'Germs!' Matron snapped back to duty. 'Cats aren't clean.'

'Don't be silly,' Tottie protested. 'Monty's the cleanest cat in town. Just look how gleaming white his fur is—the white fur, anyway, the black is shining clean. Besides, he's doing Win good, isn't he? I'll bet Win's pulse is better already.'

'That's not the point.' Matron avoided the point that had disturbed her: the patient's pulse *had* slowed and calmed. His panic attack was over.

'*Some* hospitals—' Tottie pressed her point home—'even keep cats and dogs as resident pets for the patients.'

'Well, St Monica's doesn't!'

'Too bad, this place could do with a cat to cheer it up,' Dame Theodora said. 'Dreary hole, terrible atmosphere and—' she was still brooding over her grievance—'they'll let *anyone* in.'

'I'll see you back to your room in just a moment,' Matron said grimly. 'But first—' She snatched at the cat.

'EEEeeek!' She drew her hand back instantly. A streak of red welled up across the back of her hand and began to drip on the white sheets.

'Oh, Monty! Naughty boy!' Tottie captured the cat and gave him a little shake. 'I'm so sorry. I don't know what came over him. He's usually so good. He *never* scratches. Well, hardly ever.'

'The cat didn't scratch me—' Matron stared incredulously at Winstanley Fortescue's hand, still curled clawlike, with a smear of blood beneath the fingernails.

'It was the patient!'

18

Damn the woman! No, no—not damn—he didn't mean that. Blast, perhaps. Or bother, even. Yes, bother, that was better, that was more like it . . .

Bother the woman! . . . Now that he was no longer sure who—or what—was out there listening, he felt that he must be more circumspect about his language . . . about his thoughts . . . about everything.

Nevertheless, it was a nuisance being caught up, bundled into a taxi with Tottie and carried away from The Instrument, where he belonged, back to the Chesterton Theatre, where he also belonged—but in a different way and in a different manner.

No blame attached to Tottie, though. Quickly, he exonerated her to whomever—whatever—might be noticing. Tottie couldn't know . . . He didn't know what had happened himself . . .

Besides, Miranda was back there at St Monica's, watching over The Instrument. And Sir Reginald would be arriving any moment and could be trusted to carry out tests—and Miranda's instructions—with the utmost expediency.

Miranda would whisk The Instrument safely back to the house in Merrimore Square; Sir Reginald would mobilize the best medical and psychological help available, and the process of rehabilitation could begin.

For whatever *that* was worth. What good would a human psychologist or psychiatrist be to a feline? Especially when they had no idea what they were treating?

The fact that The Instrument had scratched Matron would give them very little to go on. Probably there wasn't a doctor in existence who hadn't secretly wanted to savage a certain officious matron at some point or other. It would not seem excessively abnormal to them.

'Now you just be a good boy and keep still,' Tottie said, as she fumbled in her purse for the taxi fare.

Yes, yes . . . He relaxed in her arms, offering no opposition as she carried him to the Stage Door. If he couldn't be in St Monica's with The Instrument, he might as well be here. This was where it had all started. There was work to do here . . .

'Oh, good, Davy—' The Stage Manager swung open the door. 'Just the one I wanted to see. I know it isn't far, but I had to take a taxi because I was bringing Monty back and I didn't fancy walking any distance carrying him when he might jump down and run away. Do you think I could get the fare back from petty cash?'

'I don't see why not,' Davy said genially. 'Sounds like a proper expense to me, bringing Monty back to the theatre. There's plenty of work for him to do. I've been hearing a lot of squeaks and scrabbles lately. I think a new mouse family has begun colonizing the Chesterton.'

'Monty will see them off now he's back, won't you, Monty?' Her arms relaxed and he could feel Tottie's relief. Strange, he hadn't realized she was so strapped for cash that a few quid's taxi fare constituted a major expenditure. One she was desperate to have refunded.

All the more reason then that Tottie would never have done anything to jeopardize the show. She needed the money a good solid run would bring in.

'There you go, Monty.' Tottie tumbled him out of her arms. 'Have a good prowl round and let the little blighters get a sniff of you. That will discourage them.'

He yawned and stretched, arching his back. A good prowl around, yes. People expected a cat to prowl. No one thought twice about seeing a cat poking his nose into dark remote corners. No one dreamed of moderating their conversation simply because a cat decided to sit there and listen to it . . .

'How's Win?' Davy asked.

'A lot better. Miranda's hoping to be able to take him home after she has had a talk with Sir Reginald.'

'That's good.' Davy met her eyes. 'What are the chances of him coming back into the production? In time for the opening?'

'Oh, I wouldn't like to say, dear. I wouldn't count on it, if I were you. Not for *this* production. But what do I know? I haven't any medical qualifications.'

'I'd back your good common sense against any of them.'

'Very kind of you, dear, but not very scientific. You have a word with Sir Reginald after he's had a chance to assess the situation. Miranda is sure that if she brings Win home, he'll do a lot better—familiar surroundings and all.'

'She may be right. He'll be better off at home. Geoffrey's still pretty upset about what happened last night. If Win hadn't been in good shape, he wouldn't have survived that power failure. Geoff says there was an old boy in the other room who didn't make it.'

'It was terrible, just terrible.' Tottie shuddered. 'I'll never forget that awful moment when the lights went out and all the machines went silent. If Win had been as bad as they thought, it would have been the final curtain.'

'That's no way to run a hospital—especially not at the prices they charge. The sooner Miranda gets him home, the better.'

'Davy—' Tottie caught at his arm, her eyes wide. 'Davy, you don't think . . . perhaps . . . all these things happening, one after the other. You don't suppose, maybe, it's . . . it's Win's time to go?'

'Easy does it. He's still here, isn't he?' Davy looked down at her pale face with concern. 'You need a bracer. Let's step round to the Grub and Moth for a quick one. It will do you good.'

'I don't *want* to get ideas like that, but sometimes it seems . . .' Tottie's voice faded as they went through the Stage Door and it swung shut after them.

They've left me behind! The surge of indignation swamped him before he remembered that a cat could not expect to be invited to go along to the pub. And yet he went there sometimes. The alien memory nudged at him again: bits of sausages . . . a nibble of steak-and-kidney . . . a bite of cheese. The regulars were nice generous people and Butter-fly, the pub cat, was always good for a friendly sparring match—and perhaps a bit more, if she were in the right mood. Yes, he might drop over there on his own later.

But right now it was time to beat the boundaries, prowl his territory and see what was going on. It seemed like a long time since he had had a good look around. He started down the corridor, past the dressing-rooms, the stage calling to him like a noisy mousetrap.

Geoffrey and Peter were taking a break, discussing Peter's slightly different interpretation of the role he had taken over. They were eating sandwiches. Food!

'Hello, Monty.' Peter Farley patted the cat's head and allowed it to sniff at his sandwich, knowing he was perfectly safe from its predations. 'Like a bite?'

Uuugh! The cat retreated several paces, shaking his head and sneezing. Farley was a pleasant enough man and a decent actor—but his wholegrain bread concealed tofu and bean sprouts, thinly moistened with mint yogurt.

'That's a rotten trick,' Geoffrey laughed. 'Here, come over here, Monty. You can have some of mine.' He waved it invitingly in Monty's direction.

Tuna fish! That was more like it! Sensible lad, Geoffrey. He was tucking into a big roll literally *overflowing* with tuna mayonnaise.

'Here you go, fella.' Geoffrey scooped a large dollop of tuna from his roll and dropped it on the floor in front of Monty.

Ambrosia! It had been a long time since breakfast, and even though dear old Thea had let him eat her boiled egg, he had found that it hadn't stood by him for long.

'You made short work of that, fella. How long has it been since anyone remembered to feed you? Here, have a bit more.'

Another dollop of ambrosia fell in front of him. What a splendid lad Geoffrey was! Genes will out. Those years with Antoinette hadn't ruined him at all.

The cat paused for a moment to rub against Geoffrey's ankles, expressing his gratitude for the largesse. *Champagne and caviar, my boy, when I'm myself again. A Concorde flight to New York and a week or two seeing the latest shows, while I introduce you to all my contacts and give your career the boost that will send it into orbit.*

'All right, all right.' Geoffrey was laughing again. More easily now, as though he were getting into the hang of it after the long anxious hours of worrying about his father.

'Silly clot!' He scratched Monty's ear affectionately. 'Back to your lunch before the mice come and steal it away from you. I've been hearing complaints that they're getting in again.'

Just let one cross his path! The tail lashed furiously. They'd *dare* to approach his food, would they? But, just in case— he lowered his head and was surprised to find that the latest offering disappeared in just a couple of swallows. He looked up hopefully at Geoffrey again.

'All right.' Geoffrey separated the two halves of the roll and, scraping most of the filling on to one, set it down on the floor for Monty.

'You're spoiling that cat,' Peter said.

'He deserves it. If he hadn't broken Dad's fall—If Dad's head had crashed down on the floor without bouncing off poor old Monty first, it might have been a fractured skull instead of a concussion. He might not have survived.'

'Ah yes, that fall.' Peter Farley seemed uncomfortable. 'Tell me, what's your opinion of that newspaper story?'

'I think it's contemptible, I think it's an invasion of privacy, I think—'

'Do you think it could be true?'

The cat stopped eating momentarily and looked from one to the other with interest.

'That mark on his back—' Peter glanced around uneasily and lowered his voice. 'How else could you explain it?'

'I can't, but I'm going to talk to Sir Reginald later today. He might be able to suggest something.'

'The stage hands were working on the set that day— they still are.' A sudden burst of hammering and sawing in the background bore out this statement. 'There were all sorts of poles, slats and pieces of wood around. It might have been an accident. One of them carrying a pole carelessly . . .'

'Possible, I suppose. But no one's going to own up to that now.'

'No, no, they wouldn't. Not after what happened.' Peter sounded increasingly unhappy. 'I suppose you can't blame them for that. Only . . .'

'Only what?' Geoffrey looked at him sharply. 'Did you see anything? Can you identify anyone?'

'No, no, nothing like that. I turned just in time to see Win fall. Actually, it looked more as though he'd leapt—' Peter shuddered. 'But . . . you know . . . the media are

beginning to clamour. Davy had to fob off a couple of pho-
tographers who wanted to come in and take pictures. That's
not the kind of publicity we need.'

The cat lost interest and returned to his food, one ear
still cocked abstractedly. There was something he must
think over . . . later.

'Don't worry. Rufus will take care of the media. They
won't be making serious inquiries. Most of them know that
Jilly Zanna always tries to stir things up—only the worst
of the tabloids will follow her lead.'

'A lot of people read the worst of the tabloids,' Peter said.

'Not a bad thing. Perhaps we'll have a big rush of the
curious to the box office.'

*That's right, my boy, put the bums on the seats and the devil with
how they get there.* The cat sent him an approving glance
before remembering that it was the accident to The Instrument that was going to bring in the public—and The
Instrument wouldn't even be there to take his bows.

His fur bristled, his tail twitched, his composure vanished. Besides, the tuna was all finished and there was
nothing left but the boring old roll. What self-respecting
cat would eat that? He turned and stalked away downstage.

''Ere, Monty—' One of the stage hands snapped his
fingers at him. Another one shied a chip of wood at him.
He ignored them both.

A feeling of lassitude was creeping over him. He felt that
it would be nice to find a soft cushion to curl up on, give
himself a bit of a wash and then a little nap. Yes, that
was what he wanted. Automatically, he headed for Tottie's
domain. As well as cushions, there were always piles of soft
fabrics and constantly replenished saucers of fresh milk,
water, and munchies in one corner.

Tottie's Wardrobe was at the end of the dressing-room
corridor, as far from the stage as it could be, so that the
whirr of the sewing-machine could not be heard out front,
in case it was necessary to make running repairs during a
performance.

He was strolling past Cynthia's dressing-room when he noticed that the door was ajar. Practically an invitation, wasn't it? Perhaps Cynthia wanted company. He slid into the room and was surprised and a bit disappointed to find it empty.

No, no, not quite empty. On the chaise-longue, one of the fluffy white cushions stirred and opened big blue eyes. Malfi. The Duchess of Malfi. How could he have overlooked her?

What a divine creature. Even in his human form, he had always liked her. Now there was a new dimension to that liking. He stared at her in wonder. She was ravishing, exotic, exciting . . . and alone.

Everything that was left of Monty suddenly took over. He struggled briefly, but was impelled forward by forces beyond his control. Malfi watched him as he crossed the floor; her eyes seemed to grow larger and deeper as he came nearer.

Deep, fathomless, intensely blue, one could drown in those eyes. He leaped up on the chaise-longue beside her.

Malfi stretched luxuriously and flicked her long feathery tail seductively. She was an enchantress—and he was lost.

But—But— He *couldn't*—He made one final conscious protest before he was submerged. *Monty could.*

Monty and Malfi, left to themselves, had no problems at all. He could only stand by, as one did in dreams, both onlooker and participant in some eerie way, and wait for the episode to end.

Don't think about it . . . don't attempt to rationalize it . . . That way lies madness . . .

Perhaps he was already mad. Hallucinating everything. Everything from the moment he had hit the floor what seemed a lifetime ago. Another lifetime.

If he *had* fallen and struck his head. If this wasn't all some bizarre psychiatric episode. Who would have wanted to kill him? Been so determined to kill him that they had struck twice, killing the occupant of the other intensive care unit in the process?

And how could he have hallucinated a thing like that? Or *this?* He'd never be able to call himself a cat-lover without a guilty qualm in the future. If he *had* a future. If he ever woke from this dream . . .

19

'Horrid! Filthy! Beast!' There was nothing dreamlike about the hand crashing across his ear.

'Monster!' An iron grip closed on the scruff of his neck and lifted him bodily from his pleasant occupation.

'*Urrr* . . .' Strangled by his own skin, he could only writhe in Cynthia's furious grasp. However, it did not escape him that Malfi had streaked off and was hiding behind the screen in the corner, trying to pretend that she had never been there at all.

'Don't you ever come near poor Malfi again!' He felt a final slap and then was hurled into space while the door slammed shut behind him.

He'd never realized Cynthia had such a vicious temper. Oh, a bit of temperament now and again, that was one thing. But to think she could turn into a howling termagant like that! And after all the soothing times she had sympathized with him when Miranda was in a fury about something, making him wonder if life might be more peaceful with her.

The residue of Monty performed a neat arabesque in mid-air and set him down lightly on all four feet. He shook himself dazedly.

'Caught in the act, eh, Monty?' A burst of ribald laughter exploded around him.

His ears twitched furiously, his tail shot up. If there was one thing more embarrassing than to be caught in the act, it was to be seen to be caught. He disdained even to glance

in the direction of the unseemly merriment. He turned and
stalked down the corridor.

'Never mind, eh?' one of the stage hands called. 'It was
good while it lasted.'

Well, yes, so it had been. Malfi was a delightful little creature. He felt that she might understand him if he tried to
communicate his problem to her. Cynthia often brought
Malfi to the theatre, he had noted absently in the past.
That meant Malfi would spend a lot of time here during
the run of the play—and Cynthia would have to be onstage
for much of that time. *Heh-heh-heh.*

He suddenly realized with incredulous horror that he was
actually planning future assignations with a cat.

Why not? He was a cat himself now.

It was all too much! Thoroughly unnerved, he plunged
through the open doorway into Wardrobe and curled up in
his favourite chair. It was also Tottie's favourite chair, but
he knew she wouldn't dispossess him when she returned to
find him there.

He had intended to give himself a bath but, worn out
from his exertions, both physical and mental, he fell
asleep . . .

He dreamed of Miranda. Miranda as she was when he
first knew her, so young and vibrant and trusting, filling
the days—and the nights—with laughter . . .

Suddenly, Antoinette was there . . . and the dream darkened, the laughter faded. Antoinette, holding a younger
Geoffrey by one hand and Jennet by the other, her dark
eyes accusing him of all his inadequacies as a husband and
a father. He found himself groping for the words to make
them understand, to make it all right . . . but no words
would come.

Cynthia came instead, someone else staring at him with
accusing eyes. He had failed her, in some unspecified way.
But Cynthia wasn't the sensitive type; she was tougher than
Miranda; tougher, even, than Antoinette.

The toughest of them all was Jilly. Something moved in

the shadows and she stepped centre stage, flicking her wrist in that quick careless motion with which she had tossed back the sheet to expose him to the camera.

Women, women, too many women. Too many complications. He had felt for a long time that he should do something to simplify his life, that it would be heaven to be able to step aside and remove himself from the scene—temporarily, of course, temporarily—and just let them all get on with it. Without him.

They were dancing around him now and he crouched on the floor in the centre of the circle they had formed. He was a cat. A male in feline form. But they were closing in on him and he was helpless before them. He looked for escape . . . and there, just outside the circle, he saw . . .

Malfi! Blinking her great blue eyes, watching . . . inscrutable. But he knew she was contemplating joining the other females in the dance against him. Why? Jealous as a cat . . . that was an old saying. True, as most old sayings were. But Malfi had nothing to be jealous about . . .

Unbidden, the vision of Butterfly rose as another memory invaded his dreams. That delicious little ginger pub cat. Oh, they'd had some times together when the theatre was dark and the pub had closed . . .

Malfi moved forward slowly and joined the other females circling around him. Jealous, definitely jealous—and how many other . . . indiscretions . . . in Monty's past were there for her to be jealous of?

Women! Females! They were never satisfied. There was no escape, or peace. For man or cat.

They were closing in on him . . . His paws scrabbled wildly. The little involuntary sounds he made half-woke him.

It was dark. How long had he slept? He shook himself and sat up. His instincts cried out for more sleep, but he fought them. *What dreams may come?* Aye, there was the rub indeed. He was not going to risk slipping back into *that* nightmare.

It was dark and quiet outside, too. Had everyone gone

home? He stretched and dropped to the floor. Force of Monty's habit led him over to the corner to see what had been left out for him.

He found fresh milk and water and unfamiliar food in the dish. He sniffed at it suspiciously. Was this a commercial cat food? It seemed to be chicken-and-gravy based and he had to admit the smell was tempting. He tested it tentatively with his tongue. Not bad. In fact, quite good. He had finished it before the thought struck him.

This was fresh food . . . well, newly-opened. That meant someone—Tottie—had been in here and moving around while he slept. What about the theory that cats slept with one eye open?

But he wasn't a cat—not an honest cat. He remembered the slit of The Instrument's eye glittering white; Monty's reaction to the strange surroundings in which he had found himself. That cat-inhabited body was probably still sleeping with one eye open, while the human-driven cat was adopting the sort of dangerous human habits that could leave him vulnerable to a marauding foe.

Or was the explanation simpler than that? Cats didn't always sleep with one eye open, not when they were in a safe place with people they trusted. It could only have been Tottie moving around in here; her presence would signal no danger to Monty. He trusted her completely and so he had slept on.

Yes, that was it. No one could possibly be afraid of Tottie. Her presence wouldn't have disturbed Monty at all. If anything, it would have made him feel more secure.

There was a noise outside. He jumped, then shook himself and moved cautiously towards the sound. As he reached the corridor, he could hear the initial sound—had it been a click?—change to a stealthy rustling.

Mice? His ears pricked forward, his body quivered, he moved forward swiftly and silently. *He'd get them!* This was *his* theatre, *his* territory—

He shook himself again, trying to reclaim the feline body.

There was something more sinister than a mouse somewhere ahead. That click had been the click of a latch—
and, if the person had entered the dressing-room for a lawful purpose, why hadn't the light been turned on?

It was in Geoffrey's dressing-room. Well, the dressing-room
he shared with Peter Farley. Would continue to share. Even
though Farley was stepping into the star's part, he would
not expect to step into the star's dressing-room—not when
it was occupied by the star's wife.

The sound of stealthy movement continued. There was
not even the flicker of a torch. Someone was operating in
darkness, with as little discomfort as a cat.

*Malfi? Had she heard the mouse first and gone after it? Was she
prowling around in the dressing-room . . . alone? Heh-heh-heh.*

Begone! He struggled to vanquish the hopeful Monty's
instincts again. Of course it wasn't the Duchess of Malfi.
Cynthia would never have gone off and left her alone in the
theatre for the night. Especially not with Monty about.

Someone else was in there. Someone larger than Malfi
and with a more sinister purpose. What?

The door was wide open. So that someone could retreat
quickly? Someone—up to no good—had stopped moving
around and was standing frozen, instincts as well-honed as
those of any cat, waiting to learn what was wrong. The
someone knew itself observed, but not by whom, and was
waiting for the challenge . . .

If only he could! His claws flexed automatically and his
teeth bared, reminding him that he was not completely
defenceless. But would they be enough to drive off the
intruder? More prudent, perhaps, to wait and discover what
he was trying to do.

It had gone completely silent. Not even the sound of
breathing. He gained some comfort from the realization
that the intruder was as disturbed as he was. He crouched
lower, blinked, and tried to see what was happening.

It was behind him now! Too late, he listened to the instincts
he had inherited. He had wasted time trying to think his

way through the situation. The human mind was less effective than the feline instincts when the chips were down. And they were down now.

He twisted and shot away just in time. He felt the rush of air past him as he avoided the crippling kick by a split-second. Hissing and snarling, he skittered into the opposite wall.

No longer trying to keep quiet, the intruder bolted for the corridor and the Stage Door, footsteps echoing in the darkness. The Stage Door slammed—and the intruder was gone.

Slowly, the cat inched forward, still tensed and ready for action, all senses alert. But no one else was there. He was alone in the deserted theatre. Alone . . . and safe.

Saved by the basic instinct. The instinct for survival. Given equally to man and beast, but perhaps a bit more efficient in the beast, who knew better than to stop and cerebrate before taking evasive action.

Here's to the basic instincts! He padded back to Tottie's room. Another guzzle of milk would have to serve for the toast instead of champagne.

The basic instincts. Unbidden, the fluffy white fur and deep blue eyes of the Duchess of Malfi seemed to float before him. He stood corrected.

The baser instincts deserved their toast, too. Where would we be without them? He wondered where Malfi was right now. Curled up on the cushions in Cynthia's flat, probably.

But Butterfly was right next door. Perhaps even closer. When the pub closed for the night, it was Butterfly's time to howl. She might be outside now, waiting for a friend to join her.

He slurped quickly at the milk, gulped at the food. Had to keep one's strength up. *Heh-heh-heh.*

No! Wait! What was he doing? What was he thinking? He struggled against the feline instincts. The instincts he had so latterly admired. Now they were unthinkable . . . *unthinkable.*

'*Mirr-yeow-eow-eow*. A siren call drifted through the night outside. Butterfly . . . sweet, beautiful Butterfly.

His thinking stopped. The cat won. He leaped for the window-ledge. Tottie always left the window open a few inches so that he could come and go as he pleased. The window was barred against burglars, but there was plenty of room between the bars for an agile cat to slip through. Monty slipped, uttering an answering call to the beauty of his dreams:

'*Here I am . . .*'

20

'Oh dear, I'm tiddly.' Tottie leaned against Davy's shoulder and breathed deeply of the soft spring air. 'I am definitely tiddly.'

'Do you good,' Davy said. He wasn't so sober himself, but he felt the better for it. At least, at the moment.

The landlord had called 'Time, gentlemen, please' some while ago and they were sitting outside the Chesterfield, with their backs against the building. Like street people. Or harking back to happier times, like eager fans, queueing all night to be first when the box office opened, so that they could get the best seats in the gods to look down on their idols and cheer. Three-and-sixpence for the seat and another sixpence for the programme. Those were the days!

'Oh, Davy,' Tottie sighed. 'What is the world coming to?'

'Good question.' Davy nodded approval and went on nodding sagely. 'Good question.'

'But what's the answer?'

'What's the question?' Davy had lost the thread.

'What's that?' The explosion of decibels somewhere towards the back of the theatre brought Tottie sitting bolt upright.

'Oh no!' Her head began to clear and she identified the sounds. 'It's Monty! Monty and Butterfly again! And I had a terrible time finding homes for all those kittens the last time!'

'Beautiful kittens,' Davy said sentimentally. 'Beautiful. My little Flutterby was the cutest of the lot.' He fumbled in his pocket. 'Have I shown you my pictures of little Flutters . . . ?'

'Often.' Tottie struggled to her feet and pulled Davy up on his. 'Hurry up.' She led the way down the narrow alley between the Chesterton and the Grub and Moth into the large area they shared at the back.

'There he is—get him!'

Oh, the ignominy of it all! This was the supreme indignity of being a cat—the way humans could pick you up and toss you around. Tear you from the very loins of your beloved at a most sensitive moment—and cuff you around the ears.

'Not your day, Monty.' And Davy had the nerve to be amused.

I'll get you for this! the cat growled, lashing his tail.

'Now stop that!' Tottie gave him a little shake, then held him close. 'We have enough problems around here without you acting up.'

'The situation is improving, though,' Davy said. 'I rang Miranda while you were in the Ladies and she sounds a lot more cheerful. They've talked her out of taking Win home right away. Sir Reginald wants to keep him under observation for another day or two, but they've compromised and moved him out of intensive care. He's upstairs in the suite next to Thea's now. That's nice for both of them—they can drop in and visit each other.'

'Let's go and see him!' Tottie said impulsively.

'What, now? Isn't it pretty late for visiting?'

'That's why he's at St Monica's, they understand about theatre people. We don't start unwinding until after the curtain goes down. Win will be wide awake at this hour. If he isn't, we can always pop in and visit Thea for a while.

She's never in her life put the light out before two a.m.
Not—' Tottie giggled wickedly—'unless she's had the kind
of reason she's not likely to find at St Monica's!'

'Well . . .' Davy allowed himself to be persuaded. 'What
about Monty? Shall we shut him in the theatre before we
go? You'll have to go and close your window or he'll get
out again.'

'Monty can come too. He loves his Win, don't you,
Monty? And Win loves him. It's been a revelation to see
how attached they are to each other. I never suspected it.'

Yes! Yes! The cat rubbed his head eagerly against Tottie's
chin. There was nothing he wanted more than to go back
to St Monica's and check The Instrument's progress.

21

'There are morons—' They could hear Dame Theodora
proclaiming as they stepped out of the lift and walked down
the corridor.

'And there are damned morons! And then there is Oliver
Crump!'

'Now, now, Auntie Thea . . .' they heard Crump bleat.

'I don't know how he puts up with it,' Davy muttered.
'I'd strangle the old bat if she talked to me like that.'

'He's undoubtedly very fond of her,' Tottie said primly.
'And vice-versa.'

'Fond of her money,' Davy said. 'Listen to him grovel.
Serve him right if she left it all to an Old Cats' Home.'

'Monty would approve of that, wouldn't you, Monty?'

'Play his cards right and perhaps he could get to be sole
heir. She likes him better than Oliver.'

'Who doesn't?' Tottie peered in at one of the open doors.
'Here's Win! Sitting up, too. Win, darling—' She swooped
across the room to aim a kiss at his cheek; he hardly dodged

at all. 'You're looking a lot better. You have to be feeling better!'

'She's right, Win,' Davy said. 'You're looking about a million times better than you did when I last saw you.'

They both stood and regarded him hopefully, waiting for some sign that the old Win was there.

The figure in the chair stared back at them gravely.

'Win . . . ?' Tottie's smile wavered. 'Win, you know us, don't you? it's Tottie . . . and Davy . . . and Monty.'

He hadn't noticed the cat before. It had been half-hidden by Tottie's arms. Now his face changed; the eyes lit up, the lips curved in a smile. He lurched forward eagerly, arms flailing towards Monty.

The cat shrunk back against Tottie. He'd be happier about getting closer to The Instrument if he had confidence that it knew its own strength. A too-exuberant hug could squash a cat—or at least do some serious damage.

'Yes, Monty's come to visit you.' Tottie appeared to have her own doubts on the subject. She did not offer Monty to the outstretched hands; instead, she let him drop to the floor where he could choose for himself whether to advance or retreat.

For the moment, he sat, curling his tail tightly around his body, and observed The Instrument. It appeared to be in good condition. Of course, the hospital would see to that, in physical terms.

'Win, aren't you going to say hello?' Tottie lowered her voice and turned to Davy. 'Oh Gawd, it was easier to talk to him when his eyes were closed. Then you didn't know whether he was hearing you or not. This way, you don't know whether he's understanding you.'

'I think he is. It's just taking a bit longer to get through to him. He got pretty concussed. Just let him take his time—'

'Oh, it's you!' Dame Theodora spoke from the doorway. 'I heard voices and didn't know who'd come in. Hello, Tottie. Hello, Davy. You might as well come down and visit me. Win isn't in any shape to be his usual scintillating company tonight.'

'Thea, dear.' Tottie went through the motions of a stage kiss again, while Davy just waved a hand in greeting. 'How are you doing, dear?'

'Doing nothing,' Thea said. 'Flat, stale and unprofitable, that's life around here. I'm bored, thirsty, unamused and —just to rub salt in my wounds—they keep allowing my nephew to come in and annoy me.'

'It's too bad, dear,' Tottie sympathized absently. 'Still, it will all be worth while, won't it, when the filming starts and you're looking all rested and glamorous for your role?'

'Oh, there you are, Auntie Thea.' Oliver Crump joined them. 'I wondered where you'd got to. I just turned my back for a moment . . .' he complained to the others.

'You see? I can't have a moment's peace!' Thea stormed. 'Get out! Get out and leave me with my friends!'

'Now, Auntie Thea, they're my friends, too.' Oliver stretched a point. 'Hello, Tottie, Davy.'

It was just as well that all attention was centred on Dame Theodora and her nephew. No one saw the cat spit quietly at Oliver. Nor did they notice that the man in the chair was stirring into action.

Having gone back to staring at his hands occasionally wriggling his thumbs experimentally, he now abandoned this occupation. He lifted his head to study Monty with a perplexed expression. He was obviously trying to work through a problem, a series of problems.

The cat leaped to the arm of his chair, feeling that is was safe to do so now that The Instrument was calmer. They regarded each other quietly while the argument raged in the background.

The man seemed to shrug, then lifted one hand to his mouth. He licked the fingers meticulously, then dabbed at his face.

Don't do that! The cat's paw shot out, cuffing his ear. Then they both stared around guiltily.

It was all right, they had not been observed.

'And you didn't answer your telephone this afternoon.' Oliver continued with his list of charges. 'I was worried about you. I knew it wasn't your nap time.'

'I was otherwise engaged,' Dame Theodora said loftily. 'As a matter of fact, I was being interviewed. So I just let it ring. You didn't hang on for very long, anyway.'

'Interviewed?' Oliver was instantly alert. 'What paper? How did they get in here? What did you tell them?'

'It was a magazine,' she corrected. '*American Theatre Today* is doing an International Review feature. She *said*.' Dame Theodora's lip curled with disbelief.

'What she? You're suggesting she was an impostor?'

'Oh, I knew who she was, all right. She might have put on a blonde wig and that phoney American accent, but I recognized her. It was that newspaper doxy of Win's, sneaking in and using me to get at him.' Dame Theodora grinned mirthlessly. 'Much good it did her.'

They all turned to look at Winstanley Fortescue. He looked back at them imperturbably, inscrutably. Monty sat on the arm of his chair and also regarded them gravely; the tip of his tail twitched.

No, it wouldn't do anyone much good to try to talk to Winstanley Fortescue right now. As well try to get a conversation out of old Monty.

'He's better now,' Dame Theodora said critically. 'Not so restless. Mind you, that silly bitch would unnerve anyone.'

'You let her come in here?' Tottie was furious.

'What did you expect me to do, block her path? She's bigger, younger and healthier than I am. Also more ruthless. I must say, Win used to have better taste.'

The cat's tail twitched more violently and began to lash. He gave Dame Thea a baleful look and his whiskers twitched as well.

Catching the change in the atmosphere, the man stirred restlessly and looked around. He did not seem to like anything he saw until his gaze fell on Monty, then he relaxed again. His hand stretched out to touch the cat gently.

'It's wonderful the effect Monty has on him,' Tottie said. 'They get along like a dream. I guess the Chesterton had better start auditioning for a new cat, Monty won't be living in the theatre much longer.'

'You may be right,' Davy said. 'It looks as though Monty is turning into a one-man cat.'

Hearing the familiar name so often, the man grew restless again. The cat chirruped soothingly at him, wishing everyone would change the subject. Although the subject was one that would eventually become pertinent. After all they had been through together, could he and Monty really go their separate ways when this came to an end? *If* it came to an end? If they weren't trapped for the rest of their lifetimes in each other's bodies.

The man shook his head, as though to clear it of some unwelcome thought. He looked at the table beside his chair and very slowly, very carefully, reached out towards a small jug of orange juice.

Something wrong! The cat sensed danger and moved into a crouching position, ready to run . . . or fight. *What was wrong?*

It took several tries before the man's hand closed on the jug's handle with conviction. When he lifted the jug, it shook unsteadily and struck against the glass with a loud clink, nearly knocking it over.

'I'll do that, Win.' Tottie rushed forward. 'Your co-ordination isn't too good right now. It will get better,' she assured him, pouring the juice. 'And your voice will come back, too. You just need patience—'

Something very wrong! That terrible smell! Couldn't Tottie smell it? It made his eyes smart and his tongue curl back to protect his throat.

'No, no.' She evaded the waving hands. 'I'll hold it for you. Don't you worry about anything. Just sip it.' She raised the glass to Winstanley Fortescue's lips.

The cat sprang. He hit the glass, knocking it out of

Tottie's hand and sending it flying. The orange juice flew out in a wide arc and landed on the carpet with the glass.

'Monty! Naughty!' Tottie scolded. 'What's got into you lately? You've never done anything like that before! Are you jealous because I'm paying too much attention to Win?'

The cat crouched in a corner, staring at the widening pool of orange juice and hissing fiercely.

'*Look!*' Dame Theodora's stage whisper was more arresting than a shout. They followed her pointing finger.

The orange juice smoked and bubbled, eating its way through the carpet to the floor. The edges of the puddle widened as the acid ate into the surrounding fibres.

'If Win had drunk that—!' Dame Theodora shuddered and closed her eyes briefly.

'Hell's teeth!' Oliver Crump gasped. 'Jilly was right. Someone *is* trying to murder Winstanley Fortescue!'

22

'You print one word—' Davy spun round and grabbed Oliver Crump by the lapels, pulling him forward. 'You dare even to *hint* at it—and I'll beat you to a pulp!'

'And I—' Dame Theodora voiced the greater threat— 'will disinherit you!'

'Don't be ridiculous!' Oliver Crump fought back. 'Everyone is going to know when the police arrive.'

'Police?' Tottie swooped on the still-hissing cat and gathered him into her arms. 'What police? We're not going to call the police, are we?'

'Certainly not,' Dame Theodora said. 'That would lead to questions. Questions about all of us and our reasons for being here. That is not the sort of publicity any of us require.'

'But—but—' her nephew bleated. 'This is a murder—attempted murder. And not the first attempt at that. You can't stand by and let Winstanley Fortescue be killed just because you're afraid of bad publicity.'

'Watch your tongue!' Dame Theodora's eyes narrowed as she surveyed her nephew. 'And don't judge others by the way you conduct yourself! No one has any intention of just standing by.'

'I should say not!' Tottie moved forward, still cradling Monty. 'Win is leaving here just as soon as I can get Miranda to come round in a taxi and sign him out. He's going home where we can take care of him properly. I don't know what's going on in St Monica's, but it's not the place it used to be at all.'

That's right. A person could get killed around here. The cat rubbed its head against her urgently. *Take me home. Take me home. Take us both home.*

'Good old Monty.' Tottie scratched his ears. 'You saved Win's life, do you know that? You saved Win's life.'

He did! He did! More than Tottie knew. It was Monty's sharp sense of smell, Monty's muscles and reflexes that had saved the day. Saved himself; saved both of them. If that noxious corrosive liquid had got into The Instrument, burned its way down through tender throat tissue, as it had burned through the carpet, Winstanley Fortescue would have gone to his death. A horrible, agonizing death. *Who could hate him that much?*

The cat and man stared at the hole in the carpet, then met each other's eyes. Monty-inside-Win knew what had happened and reached out a hand to the cat. How much of Win was still inside Win?

'That's right, Win.' Tottie put the cat in his arms. 'You hold Monty while I ring Miranda. And then we'll get Matron up here and let her know that *she* can explain to Doctor—yes, and Sir Reginald, too—just why you've done a moonlight flit.'

'You know, Auntie Thea—' Oliver looked at his aunt thoughtfully. 'I don't think you ought to stay on here, either. It isn't safe.'

'Nonsense!' Dame Theodora said. 'No one is trying to do away with *me*.'

'Not yet,' Oliver said. 'But if Win isn't around, perhaps they'll turn their attention to one of the other patients.'

'Who will?'

'You never can tell.' Oliver looked over his shoulder at the doorway. 'There have been several cases over the past years of nursing staff who've killed off patients. Sometimes just because they were annoyed with them.'

Could Crump have come up with the solution? But no, that wouldn't explain the initial accident—murder attempt— that had put him in St Monica's in the first place. Once here, The Instrument had simply lain quietly and unconscious for most of the time. He could have done nothing to disturb the nursing staff.

If anyone were to drive Matron to madness or enrage the nurses beyond endurance, then Dame Theodora was the prime candidate.

'You liked that nice nursing home in Bournemouth, didn't you?' Oliver coaxed. 'You could pack your things and I could drive you down there now. It won't matter what time we arrive.'

'Why don't I just go back to my flat?' Dame Theodora asked craftily. 'I'm almost through with the treatment— such as it is—here, anyway. I can just keep on with it at home. I'd be more comfortable—and you wouldn't have to worry about anyone murdering me.'

'Mmmm, yes,' Oliver said. That wasn't what he was worried about, and she knew it.

'Or perhaps you wouldn't mind if I got murdered,' Dame Theodora's voice dropped to a low insinuation. 'Life would be a lot easier with all that money, wouldn't it, Oliver? And without having to dance attendance on an irascible old lady?'

'Auntie Thea,' he moaned. 'Don't say such things. I'd be lost without you.'

'You would, Oliver, you would, indeed. Just see that you remember that.'

Interesting . . . very interesting. He watched as Oliver Crump folded up completely.

'Well, perhaps you would be better off at home, Auntie Thea. I must say St Monica's doesn't seem a particularly *healthy* place to be at the moment—and Bournemouth is an inconvenient distance away. If you're at home, I can drop in on you frequently . . .'

'You always do, Oliver,' Dame Theodora sighed. 'You always do.'

'There now.' Tottie replaced the telephone and turned back to the others. 'That's settled. Miranda's on her way. Don't you worry.' She patted Win on the shoulder and chucked Monty under the chin—they both responded with the same slightly irritated affection.

'We'll have you out of here in no time.'

23

For the rest of the week, Winstanley Fortescue prospered. In his own home, the dormant instincts responded to the familiar surroundings. He gravitated immediately to his favourite chair and knew the way to every room in the house. He even remembered about the defective catch on the French windows into the garden and his smile appeared tentatively for the first time.

Now that he was relaxing, his mobile features began to regain their mobility. He was still reluctant to talk, only rarely trying a simple word or two. He seemed more comfortable with vowels than with consonants.

The cat watched anxiously, never far from his side.

'The rapport between those two is marvellous.' Miranda agreed with Tottie's earlier observation. 'There are moments when they almost seem to be *part* of each other.'

'Most cats have a streak of the psychic—and Monty's smarter than most, I'd say.' Geoffrey stroked the cat lying across his lap. 'He knows Dad needs soothing companionship and he's doing his bit. He's a very calming influence. In fact, he's so calming, I'm in danger of falling asleep if I sit here stroking him much longer.'

'It wouldn't do you any harm, dear,' Tottie said. 'You haven't had much sleep lately with all this uproar. It's been one crisis after another ever since Win . . . fell.'

'Do *you* think that was an accident?' Geoffrey picked her up on it immediately, but the question was directed to Miranda.

'I'm not sure,' Miranda said slowly. 'I think I was willing to believe it . . . until those other incidents began happening.'

'You still don't want the police called in?'

'Oh no—that wouldn't be a good idea at all,' Tottie said quickly.

'No!' Miranda shook her head.

Damn right! The cat regarded them approvingly. No police, no publicity. Geoffrey meant well, but if the media were to find out what had happened between the man and the cat . . .

'I suppose you wouldn't agree to hiring a private investigator, either?'

Miranda shook her head again, more vehemently this time. Geoffrey didn't know what he was asking—and she couldn't tell him. How could you put it delicately to your stepson that his own mother was the most likely culprit? Only Antoinette possessed the necessary spite—and had held a grudge against Win ever since the divorce. There was also the fact that Antoinette was so . . . delicately balanced. The increasingly erratic streak in her that had passed for high spirits in her youth was now being referred to as eccentricity in her middle years. As the years rolled on, was she slipping over the line into madness?

Miranda met Tottie's eyes and they exchanged a rueful shrug. Tottie knew.

'No,' Miranda said, as Geoffrey seemed about to protest. 'No private investigator. Now that Win is safely back home, I don't think there'll be any more trouble. We'll still keep our eyes open, but I think the worst may be over.' *Now that I can make sure that Antoinette never comes near him again.*

'Prrrr . . .' The cat gave a loud throb of agreement.

'Uuurrr . . .' Winstanley Fortescue echoed it.

'Did you say something, darling?' Miranda turned hopefully.

A meltingly sweet smile appeared on Winstanley Fortescue's face and he blinked his eyes slowly at her. He did not repeat his comment.'

'He's trying,' Miranda said. 'He's trying so hard. Sir Reginald says there's no throat damage—' Her own throat closed up suddenly. If Win had drunk that deadly orange juice . . . She was going to have to talk to Sir Reginald— it might be time for Antoinette to be put away for her own good. Quietly and without hint of scandal, in some discreet private nursing home where she could be watched constantly. But . . . would Geoffrey ever forgive her if she engineered Antoinette's commitment?

'Thanks to Monty, his throat is all right.' Geoffrey gave the cat's head an extra-hard rub and was rewarded with a thunderous purr. 'And he knows we're talking about him, don't you, old boy?'

You'd be surprised at what I know, old boy. What I don't know is who's trying to kill me—and why. He looked across at The Instrument, half curled up in the big armchair. The Instrument had been there when someone entered the room and put the corrosive substance into the orange juice. Perhaps he had even seen the deed being done. *If only he could talk.*

'Uuurrr . . .' The Instrument seemed to pick his cue out of the air.

'What is it, darling?' Miranda crossed to his side. 'Do you want something?'

'Oooeeuud . . .'

'He means food,' Miranda translated. 'I don't know what they fed him at St Monica's, but he's been absolutely ravenous ever since he came home.'

'Prraauus . . .' Winstanley Fortescue rubbed his head winningly against her waist.

'He's mad for prawns.' Miranda tousled his hair. 'Can you say "prawns", Win? You almost made it. Come on, try . . . prawns . . . prawns . . .'

'Oh dear,' Tottie sighed.

'We don't want strangers to see him like this,' Geoffrey said. 'But I was wondering . . . Madame Rosetti, the voice coach. She helped him when he had to sing for the Water Rats' cabaret and she worked to give him an Italian accent for the TV serial *Terror in Tuscany*. Do you think she could do anything with him now?'

'That's a brilliant idea!' Miranda said. 'We'll have her round first thing in the morning and set them to work.'

24

But, before the morning, there was the night.

Geoffrey decided to look in at the theatre before going home to his flat in Highgate.

Tottie wanted to check in at the theatre, too. She had rather been neglecting her wardrobe duties lately and there were alterations needed on the costumes Peter Farley was taking over from Win. She and Geoffrey left together.

Miranda drew the curtains, added a few more lumps of smokeless fuel to the fire and made sure Win was comfortably settled in front of it. A soft pattering rain had begun falling; this was a night for home and hearth. Monty, stretched out on the arm of Win's sofa, obviously felt the same.

'Fish pies for supper tonight, chaps,' Miranda told them. 'I picked some up at Marks earlier.'

Win stirred and smiled at her with a sleepy approval that twisted her heart. Fish was his favourite dish right now. She wondered if it was because fish was supposed to be good for the brain and some instinct deep inside him was telling him that his poor brain needed all the help it could get.

'I'll pop them in the oven to warm up shortly.' She looked at the television listings and decided against it. Win had shown no interest in television since his return and there was nothing she was particularly interested in seeing. On the other hand, Radio Three was broadcasting a recorded concert by the Royal Liverpool Philharmonic; she tuned in and the soft lilting strains swept through the room. Win smiled again and Monty's purr throbbed louder; she had chosen wisely.

Miranda sank on to the sofa opposite them and leaned back, relaxing slowly. Win looked so much better, now that he was home. Every day he seemed stronger and bit more himself. The speech problem was the main difficulty now and surely Madame Rosetti would be able to help with that . . .

The telephone erupted explosively, making them all jump. 'I'll get it,' Miranda said, quite as though Win had intended to answer it—as he usually did. She rose and crossed to the rosewood desk.

'Hello? What?' The voice at the other end was speaking so quickly, the words were garbled. 'Who is this?'

'Oh, sorry, sorry. It's Peter—Peter Farley.' The voice was strangulated and almost unidentifiable, obviously produced from a throat under a great deal of tension. 'Sorry to bother you at this hour, but . . . I wonder if I could speak to Win?'

'Peter, I'm sorry. I'm afraid Win can't come to the phone

right now. In any case, he . . . he isn't well enough to talk yet.'

'But I understood he was a lot better.'

'Better, yes, but not completely recovered. There's still a problem with his voice . . .' Miranda heard her own voice dip and fall. Win's voice had always been such an important part of his command of the stage. It was unthinkable that he should not regain full use of it. 'He understands perfectly well, I'm sure—' was she?—'but he isn't able to respond very well . . . as yet.'

'Oh yes, quite. I understand.' His voice told her that he didn't, but was willing to go along with whatever public statements were being issued to cover the situation.

'It really is most awfully important that I talk to Win for a few minutes, though,' he persisted. 'And you too, of course. Do you think I could come round—just for a few minutes?'

'Now?' Miranda let the doubt and faint indignation shadow her tone. 'It's after eleven—and Win has to get to bed a lot earlier these nights, you know. He needs his sleep.'

'Yes, yes, of course.' He sounded vaguely desperate. 'But I *must* see his— See him, see *him*.'

'Well . . .' Miranda surrendered to her growing curiosity. 'If it won't take too long . . .' She hardened her attitude. 'Within ten minutes—or not at all.'

'Right away, I promise. I'll be there and gone before you know it.'

But he wasn't.

An hour later, thoroughly annoyed, Miranda gave up the vigil. She had kept too many of them in her time. Dear though her colleagues were to her—most of them—she no longer viewed them through the rose-coloured spectacles she had metaphorically worn in the first flush of her career.

The years had brought a different wisdom. Earnest though certain of her colleagues were, fervent though their protestations, ardent and good-willed their intentions . . . once they had convinced their listener to come round to their view of the situation, they *did* tend to lose a certain amount of interest. Perhaps all of it. They then danced off after the next will-o'-the-wisp that caught their fancy, leaving their newly-persuaded disciple looking after them—and trying to wipe the egg off his or her face.

She hadn't put Peter Farley into that well-known category, but it just showed that one never could tell. Or perhaps he had taken her too literally when she had given him a time limit; something had happened to delay him beyond ten minutes, so he had decided 'not at all'.

'Oh, well . . .' She pulled herself up and began switching off the lamps until only one remained to light their way from the room. 'Time for bed.'

The concert was ending, too. The orchestra melted into a familiar well-loved melody. She looked at Win to see if he recognized it, as well. Something about the tilt of his head, the warmth in his eyes, persuaded her that he did.

'Remember, Win?' She advanced on him, holding out her hands. 'You were Henry the Eighth and I was Anne Boleyn. You'd written that song and you had the Court musicians playing it for us . . . just for us . . . and we danced . . .'

Softly she began to sing:

> *'Alas, my love, you do me wrong*
> *'To cast me off discourteously*
> *'For I have lo-o-ved you so long . . .'*

Win was responding—he *was!* He lurched to his feet—without his customary grace, but with an unmistakable fervour. His eyes locked on hers, he moved forward, his arms reached out to her.

> *'Delighting in your company . . .'*

She swung into his arms, leading him into the dance they had performed six nights and two matinees a week for the length of the run. Oh yes, this was her darling Win, the old Win, the Win she had been afraid she might never recover again.

'*For Greensleeves was all my joy*
'*Greensleeves was my delight*
'*Greensleeves was my heart alone . . .*'

'UURGHAARGH!' Win leaped back from her, bending and clutching at his ankle.

'MONTY!' Miranda looked down in shock at the hissing, spitting cat, who seemed to have gone mad suddenly.

Stop that! Stop that! Take your paws off her! Half-hysterical, the cat gathered himself for a fresh assault on Winstanley Fortescue.

'Uuuraaoow . . ' Fortescue rubbed his ankle, then stared with blank disbelief at the blood smearing his hand. His eyes narrowed and he looked at the cat with a distinct absence of his former affection.

Leave her alone! Don't you dare touch her! He yowled the challenge like a Tom on a back fence. He was ready to fight . . . to kill . . . for his female.

The man looked down on him bemusedly, then seemed to realize that he *was* looking down; that he was bigger, taller, more powerful than his adversary. There was no contest; he was the winner.

Don't you dare! I'll get you . . . The threat was not empty, but could it ever be carried out?

'All right, Monty,' Miranda said. 'Out you go. Out for the night.'

No, no—listen to me. Let me explain—

'Put him out, Win,' Miranda said. 'Before he scratches you again. I'm afraid he must be jealous.'

No! . . . No! . . . I mean, yes, but . . .

The man looked down at the cat and suddenly the knowledge of his power flared triumphantly in his eyes. He stooped and caught the cat by the scruff of the neck, lifting him high.

Grrrr . . . grrrrr . . . He was helpless, strangling, unable to twist and slash. And the man knew it.

'Haaa-haaaaa-aaah . . .' The famous Winstanley Fortescue laugh of triumph rang out as he carried the cat to the French window, swung it open and tossed the cat out into the night.

'Haaa-haaaaa-aaah . . .' There was a deeper triumph within the laugh and the cat recognized it as he flew through the air. It was the revenge of a cat who had been set upon by humans, wrested from his lawful prey time upon time, and hurled into darkness, the victim of the unfairness of a world in which he was smaller and weaker than the beings with whom he had thrown in his lot.

Monty was enjoying his revenge. But . . . would it stop with this?

Later, crouching under a bush in the garden, seething with fury, he saw the light in the master bedroom go out.

25

> '*Tell me where is fancy bred,*
> '*In the heart or in the head . . .*'

Madame Rosetti articulated beautifully, rolling her r's and exaggerating every syllable.

The Instrument regarded her with genial interest, agreeing 'Urrrr' and rolling a mean rr of his own when she nodded to him to try it.

'Grrrr . . . rrrr . . .' The cat echoed from his perch on the desk.

'Still sulking, Monty?' Miranda tapped him lightly in passing.

He glared after her, furious and impotent. He knew that mood of hers; it told him more clearly than words what had happened last night. He had been betrayed—and yet he could not accuse her of cuckolding him with her own husband. Her own husband's body. How was she to know that it was under new management.

He forgave her . . . grudgingly. The memory of Butterfly and the Duchess of Malfi slipped through his mind and he forgave himself, too. Perhaps the honours were even. If you could call it honour. *Heh-heh-heh.*

The Instrument turned and regarded him with sudden suspicion, even a trace of hostility. Had he caught the stray thoughts going through his erstwhile mind?

When male cats are rivals, they fight—tooth and claw. *And what about Miranda?* He felt his own hackles rising. *Interloper!* A high-pitched whine rose in his throat. *Come on, I'll tear your tail off . . . scratch your eyes out . . .*

The Instrument got up and began to lumber towards him.

No! No! No! He pulled back on the warlike instincts. They mustn't fight each other. Any wound they inflicted on each other, they inflicted on themselves. It gave new meaning to the expression 'self-inflicted wound'. He mustn't damage The Instrument—and he mustn't let The Instrument harm him.

The Instrument raised one hand—one very large hand —in a businesslike manner. He intended to do injury; it was there in his eyes.

'Win!' Miranda tried to call him to order. 'Win! Don't—'

It was time for a sensible cat to be elsewhere. He backed to the edge of the desk, still keeping wary watch on that threatening hand, and dropped to the floor. He would come back later—when passions weren't running so high . . .

He shouldered through the French window and into the garden. Mmm, the theatre . . . yes, the theatre. Time to check in there and see what was going on; say hello to Tottie and have lunch with her; watch the progress of the rehearsal . . .

On automatic pilot, he trotted purposefully to the Chesterton. A short sharp yowl outside the Stage Door, of the sort he had so often heard Monty utter, brought a prompt response.

''Ello, Monty,' Old Sam said, swinging open the door. 'Thought we'd lost yer. Miss the old smell of greasepaint, do yer? I know. Theatre gets in everybody's blood—even yours.'

What do you mean—'even' mine? He was so affronted, he gave Old Sam only the most perfunctory ankle rub in thanks before heading down the corridor to Tottie's room.

She wasn't there. Feeling cheated and slightly betrayed (again!), he sauntered over to the food dishes. Ugh! The milk was soured, motes of dust floated on top of the tepid water and something absolutely disgusting stirred in the depths beneath the dry crusting on the cat food.

Discipline around this place was shot to hell! High time he came back and brought them all up to the mark. Muttering a dissatisfaction that was as much Monty's as his, he turned and prowled out of Wardrobe and back along the corridor.

Cynthia's dressing-room was tightly closed. She was taking no chances with her precious Duchess of Malfi again, *heh-heh-heh.* Much good it would do her. If he and Malfi felt like it—

What was that? His ears flicked forward, then flattened. Instinctively, he lowered his body until his belly was brushing the floor. Whatever it was, he didn't like it.

There was nothing to be seen. In the distance, he heard the voices of Cynthia and Geoffrey resounding from the stage.

On a rising note of annoyance, Cynthia repeated a line, paused and then repeated it again. It was the cue for Win's entrance for the key scene.

'Really, it's *too* bad,' Cynthia complained. 'If we've all taken the trouble to come here for extra rehearsals, so that Peter can work himself into the part, the least *he* can do is have the grace to show up and work with us!'

Rufus said something placatory, obviously speaking from one of the auditorium seats he favoured when watching a rehearsal, since his words were inaudible backstage.

'That's all very well—' Cynthia was not to be placated. 'But I consider it discourtesy of the highest order. If not insult!'

'She does have a point, you know.' Geoffrey weighed in. 'I must say, I'm rather disappointed in old Peter myself. I thought he was mad keen on doing a good job in the part. It's his big chance. So where is he?'

Where, indeed? Geoffrey was right. This was Peter Farley's big chance—and he had too much riding on it to risk blowing it in any way.

The door to the dressing-room shared by Geoffrey and Peter was half-open, as usual. Geoffrey had nothing to hide —and nothing valuable enough to be worth stealing. Not that anyone would. Although he wouldn't be too sure about one of the stage hands; also, one could never be sure who was wandering in and out of the theatre. What with deliveries, friends dropping by, and all manner of authorized and unauthorized persons passing in and out on business of their own, it was better to err on the safe side if you had any valuables.

Perhaps he ought to see to it that young Geoffrey *did* have something valuable for his quarters. After all, it didn't look too well if Winstanley Fortescue's only son had nothing worth protecting. Perhaps a small Victorian oil painting for the Opening Night gift—

Oh yes, and how would he sign the cheque? With a pawprint?

Angrily, he marched into the dressing-room and stared around. No Peter Farley. Of course not. If he had been there, Geoffrey would have known it.

His nose twitched. There was something . . .

There it was again! This time his ears twitched and seemed to propel him towards the door, the corridor . . .

The corridor was deserted. Hollow voices echoed from the stage; they had started on a different scene, one that did not require Peter Farley. Cynthia still had a strong note of discontent in her voice.

Monty's invisible antennae were urging him down the corridor on a journey another part of Monty's instincts warned him he didn't want to take. They led him to the door of his own dressing-room.

This door was also closed; from beneath it there came the heavy scent of Miranda's perfume. *Was Miranda inside?* He had left her at the house. Could she have got here so quickly? And why?

He stretched up on his hind legs and tried to twist the doorknob with his paws. Not easy but, for one who understood the theory and mechanics of turning a knob, not that difficult either. After a couple of false starts when his paws slipped, he heard the faint familiar click of the latch and the door moved.

He dropped back to all fours as the door swung away from him and padded into the room.

'*Mirreeow . . . ?*' he called softly.

She wasn't there; a certain flatness in the air told him that immediately. Perhaps one of the other women who wore that perfume . . . But what would any of them be doing in his dressing-room?

He looked around. Something indefinable was still sending warning shudders along his spine; he could feel his fur rippling. Almost against his will, he began an exploratory prowl. The furniture was undisturbed, the costumes hung in their places behind the screen, Miranda's dressing-table—

He leaped up to inspect it. The bottle of scent had been overturned. That was why the room reeked of it. A small puddle had formed in the pin tray, dulled patches on the mirror showed where drops had landed and dried. Dried —it had happened some time ago, then . . .

Get out of here—they'll think you did it! The ancient knowledge sounded an alarm bell in his brain. Cats were always blamed for knocking things over and breaking them. Blame, followed by punishment; that was the pattern—and the injustice. With an accident and a handy cat to blame, no one was going to notice the dried-out blotches that meant it had happened a lot earlier; no one was going to ask where Monty had been then. Old Sam could attest that he had returned to the theatre only about fifteen minutes ago, but on one would think to ask him. No one cared whether a cat had an alibi when it was found in incriminating circumstances.

After the first glance, he had avoided looking in the mirror. He didn't want to see himself as he was now. For the same—and stronger—reason, he did not want to look at his own adjacent dressing-table, the dear workbench where he had so often sat and applied his make-up before striding out to the gust of applause that greeted his entrance.

How are the mighty fallen! How chastening the experiences that Life—or perhaps some sardonic mocking Gods —can inflict. So short a time ago he had sat tall and proud at that dressing-table, with all the light-bulbs ringing the mirror glowing, and casually, carelessly slapped on the foundation—

He could no longer keep himself from looking over at the adjoining dressing-table. He looked—and froze.

The Instrument was sitting there.

The Instrument . . . slumped forward . . . face down on the dressing-table . . . one hand still in a defensive position close to his head . . . his head . . . blood . . .

It wasn't true. It couldn't be true. If The Instrument was dead, how could he ever get back into his own body? He would be trapped for ever in Monty's form. No, not for ever; for the few short years remaining to Monty . . . He closed his eyes.

I am Winstanley Fortescue, a star, at the height of my powers and my profession. When I open my eyes, I will be home in bed, awaking from a nightmare . . .

I am Winstanley Fortescue . . . please let me wake up . . . please let me be back in my own bed . . . He leaned against the mirror, eyes closed, and no longer knew to whom or what he was praying: God or Bast.

But, as the dizziness began to pass, he realized that what had held true for Miranda also held true for The Instrument: there hadn't been time for him to get to the theatre ahead of the cat. Certainly not enough time to get there and change into costume.

He opened his eyes and forced himself to look across at the body again. Yes, it was wearing the Victorian evening jacket and lace-cuffed shirt of the first act finale. The scene Cynthia and Geoffrey were here to rehearse with Peter Farley.

Peter Farley! No wonder he had missed his cue. But . . . what was he doing in the star dressing-room? He knew that he would never be able to occupy it while Miranda was co-starring with him. Had he just wanted to sit at Win's dressing-table, perhaps use Win's make-up . . . for luck?

Some luck! And yet . . . he pricked his ears as a sound almost too faint to be heard came from the body. An almost inaudible gasp for air . . . for breath.

Farley was still alive! Perhaps only just. He needed help at once. More help than a cat could give. But a cat could raise the alarm—

'YEEOORREEOOOW . . .' The howl that came from his depths was louder and more frightening than he had imagined he could make.

'EEERRREEEOOWWOOOOWWW . . .' It stopped all sound and movement at the front of the house.

'EEEYYYOOOOWWEEEEYOOOOWW . . .' He could hear feet running from every direction, converging on the dressing-room.

'What's the matter, Monty? What is it?' Tottie led them. 'Are you hurt? Why are you making all that horrible noise?'

He leaped to the floor and ran to meet her. She picked him up and was pushed aside as Cynthia stormed in.

'What's that little monster doing now? He hasn't got my Malfi again, has—? Oh my God!'

26

'Someone is trying to ruin me!' Rufus Tuxford said.

'I thought it was Win,' Cynthia babbled. 'When I saw him sitting there at Win's dressing-table, and in Win's costume, I honestly thought it was Win.'

'Perhaps someone else thought that, too.' Miranda was pale but composed. It had been a shock when everyone had unexpectedly appeared at the door; more of a shock when they told her what had happened at the theatre, but she was calmer now and able to face unpalatable facts. 'Where is Peter now? St Monica's?'

'Certainly not!' Rufus was offended at the very thought. 'He's in a place where they have better security than St Monica's.'

'*And*,' Davy put in quickly, 'we're not saying where. The less anyone knows, the better, until we get this sorted out.'

'Quite right, dear.' Tottie was holding Monty in her lap and he seemed glad to be there. 'Gave us all a nasty turn, that did. If it hadn't been for Monty yowling his head off, poor Peter could have died there and not been discovered for days. Not until the next time Miranda decided to use the dressing-room—and she's got other things on her mind these days.' She lifted the cat's head and massaged its throat gently. 'You're a hero, Monty, what do you think of that?'

He gave her a loud purr. It was nice to be appreciated. Too bad it was only Tottie who was the leading member of his fan club. Dear old Tottie. He opened one eye a wary slit and looked around the room from the safety of her lap. One could trust Tottie, one could depend on her utterly . . . couldn't one?

She had arrived in the dressing-room very quickly—and she'd been nowhere to be seen earlier. Where had she been?

'Ruined!' Rufus was still on about his own problems. 'If we can't open this show with the minimum of delay, I'll have to return the advance ticket sale money. I'll be ruined.'

Quite possibly. Every publicity story of the past decade had emphasized the financial acumen of Rufus Tuxford, the famous theatrical entrepreneur who could do no wrong. They had lauded his flair for picking hits to produce, his genius for discovering new talent to introduce. They had noted wistfully, if not enviously, his manor house in Somerset, his chambers in Albany, his penthouse in New York, his flat in Paris, his yacht, his Rolls-Royce, his succession of expensive mistresses. At no point had there ever been any hint of financial problems.

Only those closest to Rufus had begun to suspect. There were too many in-jokes about his gambling beginning to circulate. And the increasing number of over-extended City financiers being brought to book by the Serious Fraud Office had proved that no one was—or should be—above suspicion. High-profile millionaires were beginning to make their associates nervous—especially when the millionaires were addicted to gambling. Nothing could diminish a fortune faster. Oh yes, the rumours, the whispers, were beginning to centre on Rufus Tuxford.

Now they were confirmed from Rufus's own lips.

'Maybe Win will be able to come back into the show himself,' Tottie tried to comfort him, unsurprised by his declaration. *Because she had reason to know?* Rufus wouldn't have dared play games with the salaries of his stars, but was he keeping the rest of the company short of cash? 'Win's getting better every day now.'

'That's true,' Miranda said. 'He's begun working with Madame Rosetti again. She was here all morning and he's made marvellous progress.'

'Really?' Rufus lifted his head, allowing cautious hope to flicker for a moment at the back of his eyes. 'You think she could coach him well enough to get him back on stage again? No one would expect a fully-realized performance;

it would be enough if he could just walk through the part. After all the publicity, the public will give him a lot of leeway for the first few weeks of the run.'

'You mean—' Miranda's voice was icy—'they'll applaud him for stepping on the stage at all.'

'There are worse reasons. It isn't as though he'd been involved in a scandal, or caught at something nasty. He just had an accident—'

'Did he?' Miranda raised an eyebrow. 'And what about Peter? Was getting his head bashed in just another "accident"?'

'She's right, dear,' Tottie said. 'It's time to face up to the fact that there's dark doings going on at the Chesterton.'

'It may even be time to call in the police.' Miranda spoke hesitantly. If Antoinette was going to be apprehended, it would be tragedy for Geoffrey and Jennet. It was better for the police to do it.

'No!' Rufus paled. 'We can't!'

'If we don't,' Tottie said, 'it's going to look awfully bad if . . . if something else happens.'

'That's a good point.' Davy carefully avoided looking at Winstanley Fortescue, who was sitting quietly in an armchair, apparently half-asleep.

'You don't think anything else can happen!' Cynthia stared incredulously at Davy. 'To someone else? To one of *us*?'

Davy shrugged. 'You never can tell.'

'But you can have a pretty good idea,' Miranda said. 'The first "accident" happened to Win. Then the power failed in St Monica's when Win was on a life-support machine. The corrosive acid was put into Win's orange juice. Now, there's been an attack in Win's dressing-room, on an actor who was chosen for his resemblance to Win, who was wearing Win's costume and sitting at Win's dressing-table. No one else is in danger. Someone is out to get *Win!*'

'You can make anything sound bad if you put it like that,' Rufus protested feebly.

'You'll have to do better than that, dear.' Tottie shook her head regretfully at Rufus. 'Lord knows, none of us want to believe it but . . .'

'Believe it or not—' Miranda's resolve hardened; Antoinette had gone too far—and for too long; she must be captured and put away—'until you take action, I am not allowing Win to set foot in the Chesterton again.'

'But—' Rufus protested. 'But—The Show Must Go On.'

'Damn the show!' Miranda snapped. 'I intend to make sure that my husband goes on!'

Hear! Hear! Lovely girl, what a fighter. Look at those flashing eyes, the defiant set of her head. There was a woman to have on your side . . . by your side . . .

'What's the matter, Monty?' Tottie responded to the sudden sad little wail. 'Aren't you feeling well?'

'Never mind the damned cat!' Cynthia snarled. 'We've got to get this sorted out. Miranda, you can't keep Win away from the theatre. It . . . it will close the show. Before it even opens.'

'That's right,' Rufus said. 'I can't possibly begin rehearsing another lead now—it's too late. Our only hope is that Win can pull himself together enough to go on.'

'No matter how pulled together he is—' Miranda faced them adamantly—'Win is not going near the Chesterton until you've called in the police.'

'It needn't be the *police* police, dear,' Tottie pointed out. 'You could have a quiet word with one of your important friends and he could send round someone who'd be discreet. No uniforms. If it's handled right, there needn't be any more publicity.'

'Or perhaps you could hire a Minder for Win,' Cynthia suggested. 'A bodyguard. That would be even better, wouldn't it, Miranda? Someone to be on twenty-four-hour guard over Win. We—we could tell people he's a male nurse. Everyone will believe that—they know Win has been ill.'

'Win has not been ill,' Miranda corrected. 'He has been half-killed. And the killer seems determined to finish the job.'

'All the more reason for a bodyguard.' Rufus was becoming enthusiastic about the idea.

'*And* a police investigation,' Miranda persisted.

'Oh yes. Yes, of course.' Rufus had the false note in his voice that meant he wasn't really going to do anything about the situation. Tell them what they want to hear— and then forget it; that was Rufus when he didn't want to do something.

The telephone shrilled abruptly, startling them all. Tottie rose to answer, letting Monty spill to the floor. He gave her an injured look and stalked over to sit at Win's feet.

'Don't—' Miranda stopped her with an abrupt gesture. 'Not until we know who it is. I've left the answering machine on.'

The machine cut in on the fourth ring: 'This is the residence of Winstanley Fortescue and Miranda Everton—' The voice on the tape was Win's, easy and commanding, in the full flow of his powers. Tottie choked back a sob as she glanced at him sitting there so still.

'I'm afraid neither is available at the moment. If you will leave your name and number with your message, one of us will get back to you as soon as possible.' There was a pause and the long note bleeped.

'Win? Miranda? You might just as well answer—I know you're there.' It was Jilly.

'Damn the woman!' Miranda's lips tightened.

'I've heard the latest, you know. I have my sources.'

'I'll find out who,' Rufus grated. 'And I'll kill him! Or her!'

'They tell me there's no one at the theatre who can make a statement, so I've rung you. You'd better have someone get back to me with all the details or I'll run the story the way I have it now. You might not like that very much.'

'*You* let us in for this, Win.' Miranda looked at her husband without favour. 'Couldn't you have had better taste than to take up with *her?* You're no better than Monty!'

The hulk of Winstanley Fortescue beamed at her uncomprehendingly. The cat flinched.

This is where I came in. With momentary hope, the cat closed his eyes and repeated his mantra: *I am Winstanley Fortescue, a star, at the height of my powers and my profession. When I open my eyes, I will be home in bed, awaking from a nightmare . . . In my own bed, in my own body . . .*

He opened his eyes on the thick grey woollen socks covering the Fortescue ankles. He recognized the careful darn with which Tottie had repaired a small hole. A bleak despair settled over him.

'And Miranda—' Jilly was still talking. 'You *are* taking very good care of Win, aren't you? We wouldn't want to lose him.'

'We wouldn't mind losing *you*,' Tottie said to the sudden silence from the answering machine.

'Don't call us, we'll call you,' Davy agreed.

'It isn't funny,' Rufus said. 'That woman can make trouble. Serious trouble.'

'She already has,' Miranda reminded him. The cat flinched again, but no one noticed.

'I'll ring her later,' Rufus decided. 'Ask her to lunch tomorrow. Have a talk with her.'

'Sooner you than me,' Davy muttered.

'If Win *does* come back to the show—' Miranda was intent on an issue more important to her than Jilly—'he's not going up that stepladder again.'

'No, no,' Rufus agreed quickly, scenting victory. 'Wouldn't dream of it. We'll change the script so that Geoffrey is the one to put the star on top of the tree. Easiest thing in the world to do and it won't make a particle of difference to the plot.'

'I'll have to take in his costumes.' Tottie surveyed Win

critically. 'He's lost a good bit of weight. Mind you, he looks all the better for it. He'd been gaining too much lately and no one liked to mention it.'

'You think he really can handle the part?' Davy was sceptical, but willing to be convinced. 'Remember all those lines? We'll keep the Prompter on duty but . . .'

'I was surprised myself,' Miranda said. 'Madame Rosetti has been working wonders. The lines of the part are coming back to him more easily and quickly than simple basic facts seem to. I suppose it's because they're the most recent things he's learned, so they're still near the surface of his consciousness. He has to dig deeper for earlier memories.'

'Like a wonky computer.' Davy nodded sagely. 'It's all there, even though you've pushed the wrong button. You've just got to winkle it out again.'

27

Responding to the crisis, Madame Rosetti cancelled all other lessons and concentrated on Winstanley Fortescue for the next ten days. In the evenings, the friends Miranda had rallied to talk him out of his coma dropped round to put him through his paces.

It was working. Slowly, then with increasing confidence, Winstanley Fortescue seemed to be emerging from the mists that had shrouded his mind.

'Oh, he's not completely himself yet,' Tottie said, having finished her stint of hearing his lines. 'But it's a marvel, the way he's come along. When I saw him lying there in St Monica's right after he fell, I tell you truly, my heart sank. I never would have credited the recovery he's made. But he always was a fighter, our Win. We might not have appreciated it when he was fighting us, but it's stood him in good stead now.'

'Maybe,' Davy conceded cautiously, arriving to take over

for his two hours. 'The old fire isn't quite there, but there's something else. A sort of . . . calculating approach, which isn't bad. Just different from the way he originally played the part. We just might get away with it.' . . .

'He's going to be fine,' Miranda kept insisting firmly. She looked at her husband lovingly, a new note of hope and joy in her voice. She could not put it into words—not for them—but he was kinder now and gentler. The Win she had always known was there beneath the hard carapace of fame. 'Win is going to be even better than he was before the accident.'

The cat sat quietly in a corner and watched sardonically. No one asked his opinion, which was just as well, although The Instrument glanced at him frequently, as though seeking moral support. He wasn't going to get it; not so long as he insisted on throwing Monty out into the garden every night.

Let me get back into my rightful skin and I'll settle with you, my lad. You'd better up sticks and move to the Adelphi or the Garrick, if you know what's good for you. He allowed his tail to lash threateningly. *The Chesterton isn't going to be big enough for both of us.*

The Instrument gave an uneasy shudder and looked at him nervously, perhaps guiltily.

Yes, you. You—Monty! I know you—and you know me, don't you?

The Instrument looked away. The cat continued to glare at him implacably. Well, almost implacably, he felt himself weakening again, his anger slipping away. They were each other—and they were not; still separated by the human/feline divide that was impassable, no matter how close they seemed to be. They still could not communicate freely. They still—

'Hello, Daddy.' Jennet had arrived to take her turn. She crossed the room and, after a slight hesitation, aimed an awkward peck at her father's cheek. Another one who could not communicate freely.

'Hel-lo . . .' The Instrument was increasingly comfortable with the already-learned dialogue of the play, but when he had to speak for himself he tended to push out the words as though they were unfamiliar objects that had unaccountably lodged in his mouth. He stared at the girl then, seeming to feel that something more was called for, stretched his lips in a smile.

'Mother says she hopes you're better—and she really means it. I know she does.'

The Instrument considered this. His smile grew fractionally wider. He gave the impression of disbelieving her.

Quite right. Antoinette would hope that he was worse, preferably dying. At best, barely able to stumble on stage and make a fool of himself. When Jennet had grown older and wiser, she would know better than to convey any of her mother's wishes to recipients who could interpret them only too easily.

'Well . . .' After the silence had dragged on uncomfortably, Jennet reached for the copy of the script lying on the arm of Win's chair and sat down. 'I guess you don't feel like social chat. You never know what to say to me anyway, do you, Daddy?' Her voice was forlorn.

'You can talk to Geoffrey all right. You even got him into the production with you. I wonder . . . if I'd asked you . . .' Her voice trailed off and she looked away.

So Jennet had stage ambitions, too. Why should he be surprised? It was in her blood. Yes, and she might be as good as Geoffrey promised to be. For a moment, his heart throbbed with pride and wonder: he had founded a theatrical dynasty.

But The Instrument sat there like a lump on a log—and after poor little Jennet had confided her girlish dream to him. She was still waiting for the response he would not—could not—make. She would think her father didn't care. She would think her father didn't love her.

Frantically, he launched himself at her ankles and twined

round them, purring loudly. She looked down and smiled
faintly.

Good. Good. Keep her attention away from The Instrument. He
leaped into her lap, renewing his caresses, rubbing his head
against her chin, chirruping and purring.

'Oh, Monty, Monty!' Her arms closed around him as she
laughed. '*You* understand, don't you, Monty?'

'Urrrr.' The Instrument leaned forward, holding out his
hand to her.

'Oh, Daddy!' Still clutching the cat, Jennet hurled herself
into her father's arms.' 'You *do* care!'

'Ahh,' The Instrument agreed, folding his arms around
her.

'It's all right, I'm not going to cry.' After a moment, she
pushed herself away. 'And I'm not going to nag you for a
part straightaway. I promised Mummy I'd get through my
A-levels first. She wants me to go to University, too. I'm
not sure. Some of them have very good dramatic societies.
And if you're going to help me when I get out . . . *do* you
think I should go to University?'

'Ahh . . .' The Instrument met her eyes, blinking
thoughtfully. 'Uni-verrr'sty . . .' He nodded several times.

'Then I will!' She gave him a final hug before returning
to her chair. 'And I'm going to make you proud of me,
Daddy. I promise.'

I already am. The cat settled himself in her lap again as
she began reading Cynthia's part, cueing The Instrument
on the most difficult speech, the one he was still having
trouble with. Jennet was having no trouble at all. Yes, the
girl was good.

I'm proud of both of you. Monty, too, was doing well in the
difficult transformation. There was obviously a good bit of
Win still in there to help him, as there was a good bit of
Monty left in the cat.

*But it wasn't enough. I want my own body . . . I want to wake
up . . . I want to get back to my own life.* Again he beseeched
Bast, God, Fate . . . Whatever. He closed his eyes and

opened them several times in quick succession. But he was still in Monty's body—and Monty, with that faintly befuddled look creeping back into his eyes as he struggled with the unfamiliar demands on him—was in his.

What if it never happened? What if they were trapped in each other's bodies for the rest of their lives?

Well, *he* wouldn't have all that long to worry about it. Even, given that Monty had the traditional nine lives, he'd surely used up a few of them before he landed in his soft berth at the Chesterton. And the day of the fall had surely cost him another one. The remaining feline lifespan would pass all too quickly. Oh, it might be pleasant enough, with good food, soft laps and loving voices—not to mention the agreeable Butterfly and Malfi—but it wouldn't be *his* life.

The worst of it would be that he'd have to stand by and watch The Instrument make a hash of his own life.

Oh, The Instrument would do well enough—probably. With good directors and Miranda by his side, he would be able to walk through the parts offered—the increasingly undemanding parts, as word of his limitations got around. But he would never realize Winstanley Fortescue's full potential; never carry out the dreams and ambitions that he had still been hatching in that fertile creative mind.

He had planned to take over the Chesterton, to become Actor-Manager of the Chesterton, with his own repertory company, producing the best of the old and the most promising of the new plays. He had long realized that Rufus had been having financial troubles, more so than was generally known. Rufus was too fond of the racetrack and the gaming tables. He should have confined his love of gambling to the theatre, where it had a much better chance of paying off. And one could take out insurance to minimize theatrical losses.

Insurance! Was that the answer? It was possible to insure someone else's life, even though that person was not a spouse or relative, in fact, it was the done thing between business partners and people who had a vested interest in each other. The star of a show or film was often covered for accidents, illness . . . or death.

It was even possible to insure someone without that person being aware of it.

Had Rufus insured his life and then tried to kill him in order to collect the insurance? It was possible. He quivered with concentration. Rufus had been in the theatre when the accident happened. Rufus had been at St Monica's when the electricity was switched off. Had he also slipped in at some point and doctored the orange juice? St Monica's open visiting hours, combined with their current staff shortage, meant that security was non-existent.

The crucial question was: where had Rufus been when Peter was attacked? If only there were some way to ask. He opened his eyes and glowered at The Instrument, who had a voice and not the least idea about the way he should be using it. Even if he had, how much of Winstanley Fortescue's memory and deviousness remained for him to call on? Could he make the connection between the threatened danger and his own safety?

Look at him, sitting there chanting his lines and beaming fatuously at Jennet! Oh God! Oh Bast! Monty was bright for a cat, but not bright enough for a human being. Rather, it was the comprehension of the undercurrents of human behaviour Monty lacked; experience that could only be gained through years of living and interaction with others.

Even if he became aware of the plan to take over the Chesterton, he would not be capable of the necessary wheeler-dealering to carry it through. Not the way he was now. Rufus would carve him up and make mincemeat out of him.

Strange that Rufus had seemed so amenable to the idea when Win had first tossed it lightly into the air—as though making a joke. Rufus had even suggested a price. Too high, of course, just a starting-point where the bargaining could begin. And still keeping it on the level of a very elaborate joke. But the quick flash of greed—and relief—in Rufus's eyes had been real. So had the sudden strange bout of choking laughter that had shaken Rufus, far heartier and more intense than their little pretext of a joke deserved.

Was it because, even then, Rufus knew that Win was destined to save the Chesterton—but not in the way he imagined?

Rufus had everything to gain, plus recouping his losses, if a large sum were to be paid out on the death of Winstanley Fortescue. With Peter Farley, a damned good actor but underrated because he had been forgotten during his American years, waiting in the wings to take over the part in a blaze of publicity, Rufus had nothing to lose.

The show would go on. No matter that Winstanley Fortescue didn't. Miranda would mourn, a few friends would grieve—and probably Rufus would put a plaque in the lobby of the Chesterton to record the Fortescue contribution to the history of the theatre.

Bloody Rufus! But how to prove it? And how to bring him to justice?

The one hope was that Peter Farley would recover—and that he had seen the person who attacked him. But . . . if Peter recovered enough to talk, who would know? Rufus had conveniently spirited him away to an unknown hospital —for his own protection. Whose own—Peter's or Rufus's?

He hadn't realized he'd begun twitching and growling until Jennet put her hand on his neck and shook him gently.

'Monty, what's the matter, boy? Having a bad dream?'

Oh yes! Oh yes! You don't know the half of it. He shook off the brief moment of self-pity; there was nothing to be gained by that. He had to try to stop Rufus before he struck at Winstanley Fortescue again. The next time he might be successful.

He dropped to the floor and padded purposefully towards the French windows. Rufus had his office at the Chesterton, there might be papers lying about; something incriminating about gambling debts, if nothing worse. Papers that even a cat could disturb and carry into view, where people could read them and perhaps start asking questions. It was the only idea he had, but it was better than nothing.

The Chesterton, that was where the action was—or would be, when he got there.

28

Tottie heard the commotion as she sat hunched over the sewing-machine in the Wardrobe Room.

The howl of rage was enough to shake the rafters. The answering outraged howl was nearly as loud. The crash of wooden bench falling over, a thunder of footsteps racing down the corridor—

A black-and-white blur shot through the doorway and streaked across the room to go to ground, growling, behind the easy chair.

'Where is the bleedin' little bastard? I'll kill him!' Woody, one of the stage hands, loomed in the doorway brandishing a claw hammer. 'Where is he? I know he came in here, he always does.'

'What's the matter with you now, Woody? Put down that hammer. And don't you dare step across this threshold unless and until you're invited in.' She noticed with relief that Monty had prudently stopped growling.

'Little bastard stole my dinner, didn't he?' Woody stayed in the doorway, looking sharply around the cluttered room. 'I came back from the chipper with a nice order of cod and chips and I just put it on my workbench a minute while I went to wash my hands. When I came back, there he was. He'd torn the wrapping apart, chips scattered all over the floor and he was hogging down the cod like it was the last meal he'd ever have—and if I get my hands on him, it will be.'

'It's all your own fault, then,' Tottie said. 'You should know better than to leave a parcel of fish and chips lying unguarded when Monty's around. You've been working here longer than that.'

'Didn't know he was back, did I? I thought he was still over at the house with the fat bastard. Probably did some mischief there and got thrown out, I wouldn't be surprised.'

'*If*—' Tottie stiffened—'by "fat bastard" you mean—'

'You know who I mean. They're two of a kind, him and that bleedin' cat. Can't trust either of them with food or females.'

'I'll pay for your cod and chips.' Tottie reached for her purse. 'And I'll thank you to watch your language when you're talking about the man who keeps this theatre—and all our jobs—going.'

'I'll say what I like—and I don't want your money.' He took it anyway. 'I just want to get my hands around that cat's throat and choke my dinner out of him.'

'It would taste better if you bought yourself a fresh meal!' Tottie pushed him back and slammed the door in his face, ensuring the last word. She leaned against the door until she heard his footsteps recede along the corridor.

'All right, Monty, he's gone,' she said. 'You can come out now.'

After a long moment, the cat emerged from behind the armchair with an elaborate air of casualness, a faint surprise at finding himself where he was. He strolled over and rubbed against her ankles.

'I wish you'd be more careful, Monty,' she sighed, bending to pick him up. 'That Woody is a nasty bit of work. Win was going to see to it that Rufus got rid of him, but now . . . oh, I wish you wouldn't aggravate him. He'll do you a mischief, if he can. If he should get you alone, with none of us around to protect you . . .

'Oh, Monty—' She gave him a little shake. 'Why can't you leave Woody alone?'

Because I don't like him. The thought came from both Monty and Win, accompanied by memory flashes of tail-pulling, covert kicks, dregs of tea thrown over him. *He's a sneak, a bully, a thief—* He broke off, growling softly.

Where had that knowledge come from? He waited and pictures began drifting into his mind: Woody, pocketing an unopened bag of brand-new nails ... Woody, casually tucking a spirit level into his carrier bag just before he left for the day ... Woody, helping himself to pieces of equipment the theatre had purchased and would need to repurchase because of him. Adding to the running expenses, which were already high enough.

Duck! He flinched abruptly at the final picture: a sharp screwdriver, hurled at him like a throwing knife, so that the point would hit first. Monty had dodged it just in time, knowing it had been meant to skewer him, because Woody had caught him watching as he stole something else. It had been sheer spite, because Monty could never tell what he had seen. After that, Monty had avoided Woody and Woody had not gone out of his way to hurt the cat, but he never missed an opportunity if it presented itself. A nasty bit of work, indeed.

Of course, perhaps he shouldn't have taken that fish, but it had been too much to resist. The loosely-wrapped parcel had been sitting on the bench wafting delicious odours of crisp golden batter covering thick melting flakes of succulent cod ... No cat on earth could have walked past and ignored it.

And he hadn't had the chance to finish it. He moaned fretfully. And Tottie had paid for it, too. Tottie, who couldn't really afford to; the happy days when you could buy a large cod and chips for five shillings and sixpence were long since gone. Everything was more expensive now, hideously so, and Tottie must have expenses he knew nothing about. It had never occurred to him to inquire. She ought to be paid more; she was a treasure above price.

Dear Tottie. He turned his head and nuzzled her cheek.

'Oh yes, I know what you're after.' She misinterpreted, as usual. 'You want something to wash it down with now.'

She carried him over to the small fridge in the corner. 'I don't know how we're fixed; I was meaning to pick up some milk, but I was a bit late, so I thought I'd nip out and get some later.' She pulled out a small carton and sniffed at it dubiously.

'I don't know—' She poured some into the empty saucer. 'It may be on the turn, but see what you think.'

Disgusting! He sniffed at it and turned away. *But that wasn't Tottie's fault.* She had a lot on her mind; they all did. He brushed against her ankles in thanks and good night before going over to the door and staring up at it pointedly. Doors opened inwards. A cat could get into a room if he knew about turning the knob, but still needed help to get out.

'I wish you wouldn't,' Tottie said. 'If that Woody catches you, you're for it. Why don't you stay here with me?'

He gave her a long deliberate look, then rose on his hind legs and rattled the knob with his forepaws. Woody wasn't going to be around where he was going. Rufus's office was out of bounds to the stage hands. (For the first time, he wondered why. Did Rufus know about Woody's taking little ways?)

'Oh, all right,' Tottie sighed, opening the door. 'You'll give me no peace until you get your way—but be careful.'

He didn't need telling. All senses alert, he prowled down the corridor to the partially concealed staircase that led to Rufus's office, which was perched above and beside the stage. It had slit windows on the auditorium side so that Rufus could watch the performance and count the house at the same time; there were normal windows on the other side of the office looking out on the street. A narrow corridor passed the office and led on to one of the backstage catwalks above the stage.

His senses twitched uneasily as he pushed at the foot of the stairs. *Something wrong.* He paused to consider what. Muted voices from Rufus's office . . . nothing unusual in that. But closer by, there was a slight scrabbling sound, a strangely familiar scent, faint, but—

Gotcha! Monty's body whirled and pounced before he could think of controlling it. There was a squeak—and silence. Then he felt the surge of triumph. *Invade his theatre, would they?*

Carefully, he lifted the limp grey body in his mouth. (*No, no, don't think about that; let Monty's instincts remain in force*) and padded up the stairs.

The door to Rufus's office was pushed-to, but not closed tightly, a rim of light shone around it, the murmur of voices was stronger. A woman's voice, low, intimate—so Rufus was not on the telephone.

Don't I know that voice? He pushed against the door, just enough to let him slide through with his burden.

Rufus was sitting behind his desk, a young woman was perched on the end of the desk, her back towards the door, her crossed leg swinging towards Rufus. They were both bending over some papers on the desk, their heads almost touching. Her gaze was intent on the papers but, since she was wearing a low-cut blouse, Rufus's wasn't.

Jilly! Damn it, Jilly! What was she doing here. Rufus had been going to get rid of her, dismissing her with a lunch. That must have been some lunch! Rufus was a legend throughout theatreland for the unsuitability of his conquests—this time he had outdone himself.

With one bound, the cat landed on the desktop between them. He dropped the mouse on top of the papers and gazed at Rufus proudly.

'Eeeeek!' Jilly recoiled, almost falling off the desk in her haste to get away. She caught her balance and retreated to the far corner of the room, making retching noises. 'How revolting! Horrible! Throw it away!'

'Good lad, Monty.' Rufus reached out and patted the cat's head enthusiastically. 'I was afraid you'd deserted us for a softer berth, but you're back and right on the job. Good lad!'

'Get rid of it!' Jilly demanded. It was not clear whether she was speaking of the dead mouse or the cat. Probably both.

'Er, yes,' Rufus agreed. He looked down at the small corpse with distaste, then had a happy thought. 'There you go, Monty,' he said jovially, picking up a corner of the paper and tilting the mouse towards the cat. 'It's all yours. You caught it fair and square. Take it away and enjoy it.'

The cat twitched its whiskers at him; it might almost be laughing. It rubbed its head affectionately against Rufus's hand and, leaving the mouse on top of the papers (having ascertained that they were of no interest), leaped back to the floor.

'Get rid of it!' Jilly's tone was verging on the hysterical; she looked at Monty with loathing.

'Can't do that,' Rufus said. 'I'd hurt Monty's feelings. It's supposed to be the highest compliment a cat can pay you, to leave his kill for you. It means he recognizes you as the Top Cat and is bringing his contribution to feeding the family.'

'Ugh!' Jilly retched again.

'Besides,' Rufus said reasonably, 'there are lots more mice around and we want him to catch them. It would be very bad psychology to do anything to discourage him.'

'That cat,' Jilly said vehemently, 'is nothing but trouble!'

Strange, that's what people say about you. The cat fixed his gaze upon her and began advancing menacingly. *It takes one to know one.*

'No!' Jilly shrank away.

'Don't worry, don't worry,' Rufus placated. 'I'll fix it.' He picked up the telephone and dialled briefly.

'Oh, Tottie,' he said. 'Could you come up here for a minute?'

29

'Win, darling, *concentrate*—' Miranda pleaded, fighting back irritation. He looked so right, so normal, it was hard to remember that his poor mind was still not quite what it had been. (Might never be again—she fought that thought. It wasn't true. It couldn't be.) He was stronger and more himself every day. There were still just these odd moments when he retreated into some place where she couldn't follow and became a stranger to her. To everybody—perhaps even to himself.

He gave her that sleepy blinking smile; as though willing, but unable to comprehend quite what she required of him. She could have wept.

'Win, darling—' She tried again. '*Please*, darling—' She broke off as she met his placid unconcerned gaze. They weren't connecting. Not at all. They might as well have been on different planets. Could she spend the rest of her life like this?

If she had to, she would! She thrust away the disloyal thought. It must be even worse for Win. Did some part of his mind realize what he had lost? Every now and then he drifted off into a reverie when he just sat studying his hands, flexing his fingers and wriggling his thumbs. It was a new departure for him; the old Win had had his reveries in front of the mirror and practised facial expressions.

He smiled at her, yawned and stretched luxuriously, then rose and walked purposefully towards the kitchen.

Miranda followed, noting how much his coordination had improved since she had first brought him home. All other considerations apart, it had been the right thing to do.

She followed, although she had little doubt where he

was headed; it was the only destination he made for so enthusiastically: the refrigerator.

He opened the door with a beaming smile for his own cleverness, then reached inside and helped himself to the smoked salmon.

She watched as he dexterously rolled each slice into a cigar-shaped tube for easier nibbling. She had stopped offering lemon, fresh ground black pepper, buttered brown bread or any other refinement; he wasn't interested. The first time he had stared at these offerings with blank incomprehensions; the second time, he had laughed aloud. But it was all of a piece; at mealtimes, he was almost childlike in his avoidance of vegetables—especially the leafy green ones. They had to be liberally dredged in gravy before he would touch them. And he seemed to have forgotten all his table manners; he was re-learning them, but with an air of doing it just to please her.

Would they ever be able to go to a dinner-party again? Or give one?

'Oh, Win,' she sighed, leaning against him. 'Oh, Win, what are we going to do?'

He put one arm around her and lowered his head to rub his forehead against hers.

'Uuurrr,' he comforted. 'Uuurrr . . .'

Yes, it could be worse. It *had* been worse—when Win was lying there unconscious, hooked up to a machine, and they had been afraid they were going to lose him.

He had made magnificent strides in the past couple of weeks; it was churlish to complain because he hadn't bounced back instantly to being his old self.

There were even compensations in this new Win; he was so much kinder and gentler. He listened, honestly listened, and tried so hard to understand. He hadn't made rude remarks or insulted anyone since the accident. His intolerance had disappeared and his charm had increased. He—

The doorbell rang. Reluctantly, Miranda slipped away from Win's arm and went to answer it.

'Miranda, darling!' Dame Theodora, bearing a large sheaf of roses, stepped forward and gave Miranda a peck on the cheek, then turned away and waved dismissal to a limousine waiting at the kerb.

'We finished filming today and had our little wrap party. I decided I'd stop and see Win on the way home, so I asked them to drop me off here. They were most impressed.'

'Which was just what you intended.' Miranda closed the door behind her, smiling; she liked Thea.

'It never does any harm to impress the Management,' Dame Theodora agreed. 'You never can tell when they'll have another job going and it keeps you in mind. Not that this job was all that much. *They* called it a feature part; *I'd* call it a cameo. Everyone sends their love, by the way.'

Miranda nodded. That was only to be expected. No one ever asked for ill-wishes to be conveyed—or, if they did, the message was suitably censored before delivery. Love from everyone. Yet there was someone out there who did not love Win, someone who wished him dead. Antoinette . . . Antoinette?

'Thea,' she said, as they settled themselves in the drawing-room. 'You've known Win for a long time, haven't you?'

'I knew him long before you appeared on the scene.' Dame Thea eyed her shrewdly. 'That's what you mean, isn't it? I even knew him before he met Antoinette. We go way back.'

'Then perhaps you could tell me—' Miranda hesitated.

'Yes?' Pointedly, Dame Theodora's gaze strayed to the cluster of decanters on the corner table.

'Oh, sorry.' Miranda decided it would do no harm to take the hint. From her breath, Thea had fallen off the wagon at the wrap party and another drink or two wasn't going to make much difference at this stage. Besides, she had always had the suspicions that Thea didn't drink as much as she allowed people to think she did. 'Can I offer you a drink?'

'Since you ask.' Dame Theodora settled back more

comfortably. 'I'm on Bourbon at the moment—it was an American company, you know. If you haven't any, Scotch will do.'

'We have Bourbon.' Miranda gave her a generous measure. On second thought, she poured one for herself. From the kitchen, she heard the snick of the refrigerator door opening and closing again. Good. It meant Win was fully occupied for a while.

'Thea, do you remember that newspaper story? About Win's . . . accident?'

'The one written by that creature who was always skulking around? I remember. At least, she didn't write any more like that. Just as well she never knew about the orange juice. What did you do, slam a writ on her?'

'Rufus took care of it, I'm not sure how. What I was wondering was . . . I mean, you've known Win for a long time, from the very beginning of his career. Can you think of . . . anyone . . . way back then . . . who might have hated him enough to kill him?'

'Practically everyone he ever worked with. He was a pushy little swine.' Dame Theodora took a long drink. 'But that's the nature of The Profession. Lots of fights, lots of feuds, lots of jockeying for position—and then it's all over and forgotten and we're all off on to other jobs. If you're asking me whether Win ever did anything bad enough to make a mortal enemy who'd come back at him all these years later and try to kill him, the answer has to be no. Not that I know of.'

'You're sure?'

'As sure as one can be. Despite some of the melodramas they write for us, real life isn't quite like that.' Dame Theodora regarded her glass contemplatively. 'If it were, my nephew, Oliver, would be a far better candidate in that respect, but no one's ever tried to kill him. Damn it!'

Miranda could only echo any nasty wish about Oliver Crump, but it didn't seem particularly tactful to do so. A close relative was allowed to make complaints that would be considered intrusive, and perhaps offensive, coming from an outsider.

'He's very fond of you,' she offered weakly.

'He knows which side his bread is buttered on,' Dame Theodora snorted. '*And* spread with jam—as anyone can tell by looking at the size of him.'

'One does feel that he had found his true *métier* as a restaurant critic,' Miranda murmured, adding wistfully, 'I suppose he wouldn't go back to being one?'

'Not with his sense of self-preservation.' Dame Theodora stared broodingly into her glass. 'There are too many chefs with sharpened cleavers waiting for him—and he knows it.'

'That's it, you see.' Miranda threw tactfulness to the winds. 'I can quite understand anyone's wanting to murder Oliver—but I don't know why anyone should want to murder Win.'

'Mmm . . .' Dame Theodora shot her an oblique glance. 'From the way you were tiptoeing around it earlier, I thought you had a good idea why one person, at least, might want to murder Win. And I wouldn't be so sure you're wrong.'

'You think . . . Antoinette? Then you *do* know something!'

'Only that the woman is unstable. Perhaps dangerously so. That's not to say she'd kill . . . deliberately. But they were all accidents, weren't they?'

'Not all of them,' Miranda said. 'The acid in the orange juice had to be premeditated. And Peter Farley was bludgeoned almost to death.'

'What?' Dame Theodora gasped. 'I hadn't heard that.'

'They're trying to keep it quiet. He was in Win's dressing-room when he was attacked from the back—and he was wearing Win's costume.'

'That's it, then.' Dame Theodora sighed deeply. 'I've known leading ladies who were no more stable than Antoinette—but they channelled it into their work and went on to win awards. But—' she met Miranda's eyes—'I'm afraid it's time they got the butterfly-net over Antoinette.'

30

'Just because you caught it,' Tottie said severely, 'you needn't think I'm going to let you eat it.'

Perish the thought! He shuddered delicately. *And yet* . . . A strange, not unpleasant fragrance called to him from the tissue-shrouded corpse in Tottie's hand. His nose twitched and he thrust it nearer . . .

'No!' Tottie thrust it away again. 'It's probably full of germs and terrible for your digestion. You only think you're interested. You come with Tottie and I'll open a nice tin of chicken-and-liver for you. You'll like that a lot better.'

Yes. Yes, he would. At least . . . part of him would; the other part salivated for the forbidden. *No!* Still battling with Monty's instincts—really, there were lines that *had* to be drawn—he followed Tottie along the corridor and forced his body into an indifferent attitude as he watched her throw her parcel into the waste basket.

'Just the same,' Tottie said thoughtfully. 'I'd like to know what that woman was doing in Rufus's office.'

So would he. He realized with irritation that he'd allowed himself to be sidetracked, to be picked up and carried out of the office as easily as the dead mouse. His tail lashed angrily. Even as a cat, he was being outmanœuvred by Rufus.

'Well, I'm sorry.' Again Tottie misunderstood. 'You're not having it and that's final.' She picked up the A-K of the telephone directory and used it as a makeshift lid for the waste basket. 'You can just forget about it.'

He considered tipping the waste basket over and knocking the directory off the top, just to show her, but decided against it. She meant well and he didn't really want the mouse anyway—*No, he didn't!* He was far more interested in what was going on between Jilly and Rufus in the office.

Casually, he got up and strolled to the door.

'Oh no, not again. You've just come in.'

But not willingly. Pointedly, he looked up at the door and then at Tottie.

'Oh, all right.' She opened the door and left it open. He'd come back when he felt like it. Meanwhile, she could keep an ear out for any trouble he might run into if he encountered Woody again.

As he stalked down the corridor, he found that Monty's senses were on full alert. This was where he had found the mouse—and where there was one mouse, there might be another. A nest of them in the woodwork under the stairs.

Silently and in slow motion, he glided up to the spot and crouched there, listening for the faintest squeak or rustle. There were more of them around, he knew it.

Voices from above impinged, distracting him. Tottie must have left the office door ajar and Monty's preternatural hearing had no difficulty in picking up the conversation.

'. . . what's going to happen now,' Rufus was saying. 'Win was all set to take over the Chesterton, but I'm afraid it would be too much for him, the condition he's in—'

'I thought he was recovering!' Jilly pounced on the admission. 'You mean, he's not? He won't be coming back into the show?'

'The show is one thing, managing a theatre is quite another. A lot more responsibility, decisions . . .' Rufus's voice grew wary. 'This is all off the record, you understand?'

'Oh, of course,' Jilly said throatily. 'I wouldn't *dream* of using anything that might be detrimental to Win . . . or to you.'

Not much. He recognized that tone. The two-faced little cow could hardly wait to get back to her word-processor and start writing the story.

'The thing is this—' Perhaps Rufus recognized that, too, and felt some sort of incentive was needed to keep Jilly in line. 'I was hoping to move on to television. Let Win take over the Chesterton and I'd be free to take the proceeds and link up with some friends who are starting a new production company making films for television. We might even get our own Channel in time.'

'Television . . .' Jilly breathed. It was the Holy Grail to media types; they all fancied themselves standing in front of the cameras, reading fluently from the teleprompter, smiling out at the unseen audience, the centre of attention, influencing public opinion, the new Movers and Shakers. 'Oh, Rufus, how wonderful!'

'Of course—' Rufus hinted delicately at the bribe—'we'll also be doing magazine-type programmes and we'll need presenters. People who are photogenic and can think on their feet . . . young, intelligent, ambitious . . .'

'Yes, yes,' Jilly said eagerly. 'You're so right. New blood . . .'

'Someone rather like you, Jilly,' Rufus said with surprise, as though he had just noticed that she fitted the description he had been outlining. 'I don't suppose you'd consider . . . No, no, of course not. You're probably all tied up in contracts to your newspaper. Forget I mentioned it. Pity . . . I really do think you'd be just right for the job . . .'

The rat! The clever rat! He began creeping up the stairs, all lesser rodents forgotten. *They were both rats. They deserved each other.*

'I'd love to work in television,' Jilly confessed. 'I'm sure I could come to some arrangement with the *Record* . . .'

'Of course, it's all still in the early stages,' Rufus said. 'If word were to get out that there might be some difficulty with the Chesterton deal, my prospective colleagues might look around for another partner.'

'They won't learn anything from me,' Jilly assured him. 'My lips are sealed.'

'Are they?' Rufus shifted mood. 'Pity, I'd rather hoped . . .'

There were sounds of playful scuffling. There was a

squeal and a thud. Jilly began making encouraging noises.

How well he knew those encouraging noises. Poor Jilly really worked at it with her ageing Lotharios. What a shame that so few young men were in a position to provide her with the jobs and luxuries she desired. A young man would make a nice change for her.

He paused outside the door and peeked in. How nice, they were down on his level. Jilly was lying on her back, busily removing Rufus's necktie and unbuttoning his shirt, while Rufus nuzzled away.

What a shame he had nothing to contribute to the floor show. Perhaps he could leap on Rufus's back? Perhaps he could walk up and spit in Jilly's eye? Something at the back of his mind alerted him and spun him around before he was aware of moving.

Gotcha! This one was smaller. Not a baby mouse, more of an adolescent. And alive. Petrified with terror, but alive. Just for an instant, he wondered about taking a tiny taste —purely in the spirit of scientific curiosity.

No, no! He fought Monty's instincts to a standstill again, although it was becoming harder, especially when he was tired, the cat gained the ascendant more easily. No, he would *not* eat this shivering creature. He had a better use for it.

Cats played with mice. He gathered it up in his mouth very carefully; he didn't want to damage it. This one was going to be more fun alive. *Cats shared their mice with playmates. Heh-heh-heh.*

Hello, playmates! He dropped the mouse beside Jilly's ear; she was too occupied to notice. So was Rufus. The mouse crouched there, frozen with terror.

Let's have a little action around here. He nudged the mouse with his paw and it came to squeaking life. It collided with Jilly's ear and scrabbled for purchase to climb over it.

'EEEeeeekkk!' Jilly shrieked and thrashed about, hurling Rufus away from her. The mouse raced across her face, narrowly missing her screaming mouth.

'What the hell!!??' Rufus stared down at it unbelievingly. The mouse scuttled across the room and disappeared behind the wainscoting.

The cat settled back on his haunches and regarded the two humans brightly.

'That bloody sodding cat!' Jilly scrambled to her feet and aimed a hysterical kick at it.

Missed me by a mile. He moved only slightly as the nylon-clad foot swished past him.

'And he's laughing at us!' Jilly shrieked. 'Look at him— he's laughing at us!' She looked around wildly. 'Where are my shoes? I'm going to put them on and stamp over him in my high heels!'

'This is too much!' Rufus stamped across the office and flung open the door.

'TOTTIE!' he bellowed. 'TOTTIE, COME HERE AND GET THIS BLOODY CAT!'

'Couldn't you have waited a minute?' Jilly turned her fury on him as she tried to pull her apparel back into a state resembling respectability.

Rufus looked at her blankly for a moment, then down at himself and hastily began to repair his own inadequacies as footsteps began pounding up the stairs.

Please adjust your dress before leaving. Heh-heh-heh.

'It's all right.' Woody appeared in the doorway. 'I'll get rid of him for you.'

'No, you won't!' Tottie was right behind Woody. She pushed him aside and dashed across the room to scoop Monty into her arms. 'What's he done now to get everyone upset?'

'He brought in another mouse,' Rufus said tightly. 'This one was alive. It . . . it startled Ms Zanna.'

'It ran over my face,' Jilly said bitterly. 'Right across my face.'

'Really?' Tottie's eyes widened in mild disbelief. 'How did Monty get a mouse up to your face?'

'Never mind that now—' Rufus said quickly.

'I'm sorry, Rufus,' Jilly said at the same time. 'I want to go home and stand under the shower for about an hour. Ring me tomorrow and we can get together and . . . continue our discussion.' She gave Monty a venomous look. 'Without the cat.'

'Oh dear, she *is* upset,' Tottie said, as Jilly's footsteps clattered angrily down the stairs. 'Monty, you *are* a naughty boy.'

'Just get him out of here!' Rufus snapped.

'Let *me* take care of him,' Woody growled, reaching out to snatch at the cat. 'I'll guarantee he never gives us any more trouble.'

The cat growled back from the safety of Tottie's arms and slashed out at the clutching hands.

Cursing, Woody leaped back. Long thin ribbons of red welled up and ran down one hand.

'You sodding bastard!' he snarled. 'I'll get you for that!'

'You can get out of here, too!' Rufus was at the end of his patience.

Tottie waited until she heard Woody's footsteps die away before she went to the door. She smiled over her shoulder at Rufus, but he seemed sunk in a foul mood, glaring down at the carpet darkly.

'I think I'll take you back to the house now for your own protection,' she murmured in Monty's ear as she carried him down the stairs. 'No matter how many mice you've caught, you haven't made yourself Mr Popularity around here tonight.'

But I had a good time. Heh-heh-heh.

31

'Oh, Tottie!' Miranda seemed flustered as she opened the door. 'Come in.' She looked over Tottie's shoulder. 'You're alone?'

'Except for Monty,' Tottie pointed out. 'I'm not sure what he's been up to, but he's blotted his copybook good and proper at the Chesterton tonight.' She added craftily. 'He's probably missing Win.'

'Oh yes, take him through,' Miranda said abstractedly. She remained in the doorway, looking up and down the street.

'You expecting someone, dear?'

'Only Oliver Crump. He's coming by to pick up his aunt.'

'Oooh, Win won't like that,' Tottie said. The cat growled softly in agreement.

'It will be a matter of supreme indifference to Win.' Miranda smiled wanly. 'In fact, I'd feel better if Win *could* get angry, or be insulting, or do anything more like his old self. He's so sweet and eager to please these days that it breaks my heart.' Miranda stepped back and closed the door.

'I know what you mean, dear.' Tottie nodded sagely. 'It was the same when the children were ill. You begin to wish they'd do something awful, just so you'd know they were getting better.'

'If that's the criterion,' Miranda said drily, 'then I can tell you Thea is feeling *very* well.'

'Oh dear! It's like that, is it?' Tottie had no illusions about what she meant. 'Problems?'

'Not ours,' Miranda said. 'Oliver's problem—when he arrives.'

'I thought she had that film job. She's usually all right when she's working.'

'It finished today. She came straight here from the wrap party.'

'Oh.' Tottie had the full picture now. 'And I suppose you were your usual hospitable self?'

'Too much so, I'm afraid. I didn't realize—'

'No one ever does. She's awfully clever about it. Oh, well, you say Oliver's on the way—?'

'He rang when he couldn't reach her on the set. Some of the crew knew where she'd gone. He'll be here any minute.' Miranda sighed. 'I suppose he'll be annoyed with me—and rightly so, I'm afraid.'

'You weren't to know,' Tottie soothed. 'I'll stick around. He won't create so much if someone else is present.'

'Oh, Tottie, you're a darling.' Miranda smiled warmly. 'Stay the night—please.' Suddenly, she found herself limp with relief; a friendly companion by her side to share the burden—that was what she needed. What Win had once been, but now . . . 'Win's—I don't know. Thea seems to have thrown Win into an odd mood.'

'Don't you worry, dear.' Tottie was gratified. 'We'll calm him down again . . . oh dear!'

'And so—' Dame Theodora was on her feet, acting out an elaborate anecdote. Win, semi-reclining on the sofa, was grinning at her with appreciation, egging her on.

'And so—' Dame Theodora flourished the sheaf of roses she was using as a prop. 'She threw the coffee in his face!'

'Griyte! Griyte!' The Instrument applauded.

'You should have *seen* him. Even with the coffee dripping down his chops, he couldn't believe it. *He's* usually the one to behave badly!'

'Miykes a chiynge, dunnit?' The Instrument said.

'Oh, Win, you *are* a fool!' Dame Theodora collapsed back on to her sofa, laughing uproariously, and reached for her drink.

'But—' Tottie gave Miranda a worried look and lowered her voice—'why does he keep using a Cockney accent?'

'Just wait a minute,' Miranda answered *sotto voce*. 'Win, darling.' She raised her voice. 'Here are Tottie and Monty to see you.'

'Guid! Guid!' The Instrument switched to Scots. 'Hullo, ma darrlings.' He beamed at them with an air of enjoying his own cleverness.

'He's been like this since Thea arrived,' Miranda murmured. 'I never know what accent will come out next—

and she thinks it's funny. It . . . it's beginning to frighten me. Do you think it might be a new symptom? Perhaps he's heading for a relapse?'

'I don't think so, dear.' Tottie's tone didn't ring true; she was worried, too. 'Before, he didn't talk at all.'

'Von't you haff somesing to drink?' It was German now; in fact, a line from an all-but-forgotten film. With luck, audiences would have forgotten it completely, but it appeared that vestiges of it remained in The Instrument's memory.

Shades of Eliza Doolittle! The cat sank down on his haunches and shook his head groggily, recognizing what must be happening. Monty, desperately trying to do what was required of him, was striking out on his own conversationally. He couldn't be blamed for that; trapped in the alien body for heaven knew how long, he had learned to manage it pretty well, but the voice production was still a problem to him. Scrabbling frantically through The Instrument's memory, he was catching and throwing out ready-made phrases and tag-lines as he found them, not realizing that they came equipped with accents pertaining to the particular role. Monty had not quite grasped that Winstanley Fortescue should utter words in his own ordinary standard English accent.

'I think I will have a drink.' Tottie sounded overcome.

'Reet, help thasel' to summat, lass.' He beamed at her again.

'Oh dear,' Tottie said. 'Madame Rosetti has her work cut out for her.'

'She's done wonders so far.' Miranda poured out a drink for Tottie and, in response to Dame Theodora's subliminal signal, refreshed that glass. 'He's almost flawless in the part now. It's just when he begins to talk normally that he's like this. Normally!' She gave a faintly hysterical laugh.

The Instrument glanced over at her uneasily, as though fearful that he had done something wrong.

'Everything all right, darling?' she asked, giving him a reassuring smile.

'Oh, I say, old gel,' he drawled. 'Absolutely spiffin'.'

'He got it almost right that time,' Tottie said. 'At least, he's making an effort.'

The doorbell pealed sharply. Miranda went to answer it.

'That will be for me, I fear,' Dame Theodora said dramatically. 'The tumbril awaits!'

'It is a far, far better thing I do—' The Instrument responded instantly to the cue—'than I—*aaargh*!'

Unable to control himself any longer, the cat had taken a severe nip at an ankle.

'Monty!' Tottie swooped and gathered him up, retreating with him as Winstanley Fortescue rubbed his ankle and glared at the cat. 'What's got into you tonight? I thought you'd be all right over here. I'm sorry, Win. Monty's been out of sorts all day.'

The Instrument glowered, but thankfully produced no remark. If he would only retreat into brooding silence— and stay there between performances—the situation might be saved. A brooding semi-invalid was understandable; but a Winstanley Fortescue roaming around making inane remarks in a variety of inappropriate accents would simply be making a fool of himself. No matter how well he did on stage, even fewer parts would be offered in future.

Miranda's voice rang out in the front hall on a higher, more artificial note than she used to intimates. More than one voice answered her; there was a concerted rumble, as of introductions or explanations. She returned with Oliver Crump immediately behind her and a large unknown man following.

'I knew it was you,' Dame Theodora said. 'Every time I'm enjoying myself, you come along and try to spoil it. I see you've brought reinforcements. Afraid to face me alone?'

'This has nothing to do with you, Auntie Thea.' Oliver Crump glanced at her glass and glanced away again, not prepared to make an issue of it. 'I'm doing a favour for Rufus, that's all.'

'A *favour* for Rufus? From you?' Dame Theodora shook her head. 'Most unlikely.'

'Nevertheless, Auntie Thea, it's true. Rufus rang me because he knew I had, er, experience, with certain difficulties and he needed the benefit of my advice on the subject. Naturally, I was most happy to be of help. That's why I've brought Ace along tonight. Rufus asked me to.'

'Ace?' Dame Theodora looked over Oliver's shoulder at the large man looming behind him. 'Don't I know you?'

'Good evening, Dame Theodora.' The man's voice was deep and surprisingly pleasant. 'We met a few years ago when I was doing a job for Mr Crump.'

'When you were minding him, you mean. I remember.' Dame Theodora's eyes lit with delight. 'There was a rumour going round that some American restaurant chain had put out a contract on Oliver because of the way he reviewed their flagship restaurant—'

'People in catering have no sense of humour.' Oliver shuddered. 'It's being cooped up in hot kitchens in all weather, with all sorts of dangerous weapons around, I suppose. Their thoughts naturally turn to violence.'

'You were Oliver's shadow for about six months,' Dame Theodora recollected. 'Until he chickened out and got a job as theatre critic.'

'It pays better,' Oliver defended huffily. 'And there's less dyspepsia.'

'For you, perhaps—but not for your victims. Anyway—' the light in her eyes dimmed—'there wasn't any truth in the rumour—you're still here.'

'Maybe that's because I'm a very good minder,' Ace Barron said. 'I could show you my references, but I think my best reference is the fact that all my clients are still alive and healthy.'

'That's what I told Rufus,' Oliver said, 'and it was good

enough for him. Ace is going to look after Win for the next couple of weeks.'

'For as long as necessary,' Miranda corrected sharply. 'Rufus isn't going to fob us off by providing security for a limited time and then depriving Win of it just when he may need it most.'

'We talked about that,' Oliver said. 'But Rufus believes —and I must say, I agree with him—that the incidents have been intended to stop the production, rather than aimed at Win personally. After *Serpent in the Heather* has opened, there shouldn't be any more trouble.'

'Why should anyone want to stop the show from opening?'

'Because it's based on a little-known real-life poisoning case which was unsolved—and it presents a solution involving someone not even suspected at the time. That's always a dangerous thing to do.'

'That's ridiculous,' Miranda said. 'Besides, there were no descendants from anyone in that family. The author assured us of that.'

'I'm afraid the author lied,' Oliver said. 'I've been doing some research at the Newspaper Library in Colindale and reading up the case in the Edinburgh newspapers of the time. There is every reason to believe that the son, the wife who married again a second time and the American visitor all had subsequent issue. If Rufus wants to follow this up, he can set a research assistant to work on the genealogies concerned.'

'But why should anybody worry about it after all this time?' Tottie wanted to know.

'Ah, but time doesn't matter,' Oliver said. 'Remember —there is no Statute of Limitations on murder.'

'Perhaps not,' Dame Theodora said, 'but all the people directly involved will be dead by this time. Why should their children or great-grandchildren worry about what their ancestors did?'

'It might have a bearing on their inheritance.' Oliver

looked wise. 'A murderer isn't allowed to profit from his or her crime. If they had profited, it's possible that the inheritance can be taken away from the heirs and redistributed in the light of new knowledge.'

'I wouldn't like to see anyone try it.' Dame Theodora was nothing if not practical. 'It's also possible that whatever money there once was has long since been spent.'

'It's an ingenious theory.' Miranda's tone implied that Oliver had sat through too many thrillers. 'But I suspect that any half-competent lawyer could make hash of any attempt to take money away from the heirs of the heirs. Stopping the production isn't a good enough reason to kill someone.' No, it might be comforting to think that this wasn't a personal vendetta against Win, but she didn't believe it. Someone was out to get him—and she must quietly suggest to Ace Barron that he keep an especially sharp eye on Antoinette.

'They could get the same effect more easily by burning down the theatre.' Dame Theodora laughed abruptly. 'Oh, Oliver, you're such a fool you quite cheer me up!'

I'll still bet my munchies on Rufus himself. Clever devil, encouraging Oliver to line up a few remote and amorphous figures upon whom suspicion could be thrown, if necessary. He'd take no bets at all on Rufus's paying out any fees for a research assistant to waste time rootling through old records in search of phantoms. Rufus would rather throw his money away on the turn of a card.

'Always glad to amuse you, Auntie Thea.' Oliver spoke between clenched teeth. 'It's nice to be appreciated—even for the wrong reasons.'

'Anyway, Oliver,' Miranda said quickly, 'thank you so much for finding Ace for us. It was so kind of you. And of Rufus.'

And that was another thing. Why was Rufus being so cooperative? Could Ace really be trusted to look after The Instrument properly? A friend of Oliver's? Paid by Rufus? If it came to the crunch, whose side would he really be on?

'Glad to be of help.' Oliver relaxed in the warmth of Miranda's gratitude. 'I knew you'd like Ace—and he'd like you.' He glanced uneasily at Winstanley Fortescue, who had been silently watching the scene. 'What do you think, Win?'

'Mr Fortescue—' Ace advanced on him, hand outstretched. 'I'm sure we're going to get along well. Don't you worry, I'll look out for you.'

The Instrument allowed his hand to be seized and shaken. He glowered at Monty and moved his ankles to a more inaccessible position.

'Fair dinkum, cobber?' he growled.

32

With Ace Barron unobtrusively standing by, Winstanley Fortescue returned to the Chesterton and joined in the rehearsals. Gradually, life returned to a semblance of normal and the show began to take shape again. The occasional news about Peter Farley was encouraging, if not quite so good as might be desired: he was recovering slowly, but not fit to do any talking yet. If people had their own opinions as to whether or not this was the truth, they kept them to themselves.

'I don't know,' Rufus said moodily at the end of the week. 'Something seems to be missing. It's not quite right.'

'Is it ever?' Davy asked. 'What's missing is the audience. Once they see faces out there in the auditorium, the cast will perk up no end.'

'You may be right.' But Rufus narrowed his eyes at the way Winstanley Fortescue was slumped in an armchair, half-asleep now that his scene was over.

'Oh, I *do* still worry about Win, dear.' Tottie ventured a mild criticism. 'Look at him, sitting there like a puppet with its strings cut every time he's not in a scene. You don't think you're working him too hard, do you?'

'He's conserving his energy,' Davy said, with more certainty than he felt. 'Don't worry about Win, he's a pro to his fingertips. He'll be all right on the night.'

'We don't have much choice, anyway,' Rufus said. 'We're opening next Wednesday. What the hell—' He slapped his hands together decisively. 'I've bet on longer odds than this!'

'Dress Rehearsal this afternoon, Win.' Miranda smiled brightly at her husband.

'Oh—' He seemed to grope for a reply—or perhaps the proper accent in which to convery it. Madame Rosetti had been keeping his vocal cords to the grindstone; perhaps too much so, he was beginning to develop a faintly haunted look in his offstage hours.

'Oh, good.' He waited to see if this was the right response.

'I've arranged an impromptu little party afterwards,' Miranda went on. 'Quite apart from the Opening Night party, I mean. That will be Rufus's. This will be ours, our thanks to the cast and backstage staff for all their help and patience. It ought to cheer them all up.'

'Oh. Good.'

'I knew you'd be pleased.' Miranda kept her smile bright. Would Win ever speak in polysyllables again? 'I've ordered all your favourite foods. And champagne.'

'Oh. Good.' He held out his arms to her with that melting smile, and she duly melted. Did words matter all that much, after all? Here was the real Win and he needed her as he had never needed her before. Everything else would follow . . . in time.

'I do wish you'd stop prowling around and *settle*,' Tottie scolded. 'There are no hot bricks around here, although you act like you're dancing on them. Come on now, Monty, give it a rest. It's wearing me out, just watching you.'

Then stop watching me! That was the trouble with this place: no privacy anywhere. They were all watching each other with varying degrees of mistrust. The Minder was watching everyone. Would the killer try to strike at Winstanley Fortescue again before the opening?

It was already Dress Rehearsal; the Opening was tomorrow night. He had every right to be nervous. He had to be vigilant and ready to protect The Instrument from the danger that might strike from any quarter. Absently, he sharpened his claws on one of the sawhorses that had been set up in the foyer.

'Don't *do* that!' Tottie aimed a half-hearted blow at him.

He didn't bother to dodge; she had no intention of hitting him.

'Here we are, Tottie.' Two of the stage hands appeared, carrying the long boards that were to be set across the sawhorses to make a trestle table.

'Fine. Just put them there.' Tottie gestured unnecessarily; they knew what was to be done. She held the long length of material that was going to double as a tablecloth all ready to spread out over the boards. 'The caterers will be arriving any minute.'

Caterers? A party? The cat retracted his claws and moved away as the stage hands set up the table and Tottie covered it. *Why were they getting ready so early?* The Opening wasn't until tomorrow night and the public would be thronging the foyer. The table would be in everybody's way. And the caterers shouldn't be arriving tonight. The party should be held backstage after the performance, as usual. The food would spoil—or be very tired—if it was going to hang around for twenty-four hours. What was going on?

Someone rattled the main entrance doors and Tottie went to open them. A small procession filed in bearing film-shrouded trays of buttered rolls and fancy breads, platters of sliced roast beef, smoked salmon, chicken and ham; bowls of potato, rice, three-bean and green salads.

'Don't just stand there,' Tottie directed the stage hands. 'Go and help them bring everything in.'

The augmented procession continued, with bottles of champagne borne in, along with ice buckets, trays of petits-fours, cheesecakes, gâteaux, fruit salad, coffee urns. They were all distributed along the table. A groaning board, indeed.

The cat backed into a corner, forgotten, and watched the preparations, salivating.

Oh yes, it was a party. Tonight. He closed his eyes in ecstasy. *He loved parties.*

The *pièce de résistance*, an enormous bowl of caviar in a bed of ice, was placed in the centre of the table. Fragrant aromas seeped from beneath the plastic wrapping with promise of tasty titbits to come from his friends.

Uuugh! Another smell violated his delicate nostrils. Ugly, appalling, vile—he hardly needed to open his eyes to know that Woody had appeared on the scene.

'What's all this, then?' Woody demanded.

'Oh yes.' Tottie faced him. 'Trust you to come along when all the work's done.'

'What work? Nobody told me anything.'

'It's a surprise party. Miranda and Win are giving it for everyone. To cheer us all up before the Opening.'

'Huh!' Woody grunted. 'Think they can buy friends, do they?'

Ugh! He was a ghastly creature! Stupid and uncouth—and he smelled of horrible things. Hatred and turpentine and paint stripper and—

Ugh! The cat retreated from the abomination until he was crouched against the wall. Woody *reeked* of *dog!*

There was a shout from the auditorium.

'That's the scene change coming up,' Tottie said. 'You'd all better get in there and do your stuff. Not a word of this, mind you. Miranda wants it to be a surprise.'

Dear Miranda . . . always so sweet and thoughtful. How typical of her. So generous to her friends—our friends. Our dear sweet friends ... now there was a thought ... a party for our friends ...

He watched Tottie make a few minor adjustments to the table arrangement, then bestow permission on the catering staff to slip inside the auditorium for a sneak preview of the show.

They would all be completely absorbed until the end of the Dress Rehearsal. At least another hour ... *Heh-heh-heh.*

'Oh God!' Cynthia shrieked. 'The cats are in the caviar! That's disgusting!'

Who paid for it, for Bast's sake? Monty raised his head and glared at her briefly.

'One of them's yours,' Tottie pointed out. 'You can't talk.'

The Duchess of Malfi gulped greedily at the caviar without looking up to respond to the voice she knew so well. Butterfly quivered, but also stood her ground, such delicacies did not come her plebeian way often.

'Oh no!' Miranda was half way between laughter and tears. She had wanted everything to be so perfect.

Geoffrey quickly turned a laugh into a cough.

'That cat!' Rufus groaned. 'That bloody cat!'

Just returning a bit of hospitality. What's wrong with that? My dear little ladies are as entitled to a party as you are—perhaps more so.

'Filthy beasts!' Woody started forward menacingly. 'I'll take care of them!'

Winstanley Fortescue gave a sudden hoot of laughter and charged forward to join the friends he recognized as his. He bumped into Woody and sent him flying without even noticing that he had done so. Woody cursed him.

Butterfly and Malfi moved over unconcernedly to make room for The Instrument to join them, recognizing in some mysterious female way that, although he was in an unfamiliar form, he was not unknown to them.

The Instrument thrust one finger into the rapidly depleting bowl of caviar and brought out a generous dollop. He started to lick at it but, meeting Monty's censorious eye, he changed his mind and thrust it into his mouth.

'That's right, Win.' Miranda was becoming adept at covering for these outbreaks of eccentricity. 'It's a staff party! And Monty is part of the backstage staff. Why shouldn't he invite his friends to join us?'

Giggles broke out from the watching crowd; the ice was broken and everything was a joke.

'Oh, well,' someone said. 'There's lots of other goodies.' They broke ranks and advanced on the table.

'That's right,' Rufus said resignedly. 'There'll be more caviar tomorrow—and we'll keep a better guard on it.'

33

'They say a bad Dress Rehearsal means a good Opening,' Tottie sighed. 'But it wasn't really bad enough to be bad—'

'Or good enough to be good,' Davy agreed. 'All we can do is hope for the best.' He frowned. 'I just wish I didn't have the feeling that Win is . . . well, losing interest. As though, at any performance, he might just stroll offstage and go somewhere else. The way Monty does when he's lost interest in whatever he's doing.'

Bast damn it! It was only too possible. More so than Davy knew. It was a problem he had noticed in himself. Monty's attention span was limited and his own attempted concentration on a subject was too often over-ruled by the cat's desire to curl up and sleep or go and satisfy his curiosity about what was happening elsewhere.

'All I'm going to worry about right now is tonight's performance,' Tottie said firmly. 'The rest of the run can take care of itself.'

There was the familiar air of supercharged excitement backstage; the build-up of tension and near-hysteria which would find release when the house lights dimmed, the curtains parted, and the performance began. For good or ill.

The Stage Door opened and closed constantly; flowers were delivered, messages of goodwill arrived, friends and hangers-on popped in 'just for the teeniest minute to wish you good luck', the Front of House staff rushed back and forth with all the last-minute errands and duties.

Chaos! Bedlam! The breath of Life! And, all too soon, the call: 'Five minutes, please.'

As the curtains parted and the applause erupted, the cat watched silently, yearningly, from the wings. Ace Barron just watched. The performance began.

Not bad. Not bad. Could have been worse. A lot worse. The cat had retreated to the star dressing-room after the performance to savour the triumph. He sat half-hidden behind the umbrella stand, his nose vaguely complaining at the scents drifting his way. *The perfumes and after-shave lotions some people wore!*

'Darlings, you were wonderful!'

'Marvellous, darlings, marvellous!'

'A triumph—it will run for ever!'

'Absolutely brilliant!'

The babble of voices was deafening. If only the reviews were half as enthusiastic as the flattery of friends, the show was a hit.

And so it should be. As the sound of applause struck his eardrums, Winstanley Fortescue's reflexes and expertise had taken over. No one would ever know how brilliant his performance actually was because no one would ever know the difficulties he had been labouring under.

Oh, give Monty his due. A lesser cat might have turned tail and run as the barrage of sound hit him. Thank Bast, Monty was a theatre cat; he had always been fond of the noise and excitement, to the extent that he had had to be actively discouraged from strolling across the stage during performances and garnering his own round of applause. Now he had it all to himself.

'Win! Miranda! Darlings! Better, much better than one

dared to hope!' Dame Theodora lowered her voice to a modified shriek in order to be heard over the background noise. 'Even Oliver liked it!'

'I liked it very much—and I'm going to say so!' Oliver Crump beamed approval.

'Darling, I'm sorry to bring the skeleton—if I can call him that—to the Feast,' Dame Theodora apologized to Miranda. 'But the show was sold out! I couldn't get a ticket, so I had to come on Oliver's extra ticket. That meant I couldn't get out of bringing him backstage to the party. Don't worry—he really *is* going to do you a super review.'

'I'm not worried,' Miranda laughed. They had come through triumphant. Everything was wonderful. Everyone was her best friend—even Oliver Crump. 'You're both welcome!'

'We'll pop along to the other dressing-rooms and spread the good word,' Dame Theodora said. 'See you at the champagne buckets!'

Oliver hardly winced as he dutifully followed his aunt.

Really, there was nothing more boring than watching other people being the centre of attention. Even when those people were Win and Miranda. The cat yawned, then looked up hopefully, aware that someone had come to stand beside him.

No, no petting or handouts there. It was Ace Barron, still very much on duty. And this was one of the best vantage-points in the room. All was well and would continue to be well while Ace was on guard.

No need for both of us to keep watch here. Besides, he wanted to look in on Geoffrey and see how the boy was enjoying this first flush of success. The cat stretched and sauntered out into the corridor.

Faugh! How could he have forgotten that Antoinette would be here? Geoffrey was her son, too. (Sorry about that, my boy— but fortunately, you take after me.)

He slid into the dressing-room, keeping his distance from Antoinette, but bestowing a friendly ankle rub on Jennet. Friends of Geoffrey were also there and the television escapee had his own coterie surrounding him. It was too crowded here; he could make contact with Geoffrey later. Well, at least, he could hop into Geoffrey's lap at a quiet moment and purr congratulations and rub his head against Geoffrey's chin. Geoffrey would recognize the affection without ever knowing why it was so fervent.

Ah well . . . even in this condition, there were compensations . . . He poked his head round the door of Cynthia's dressing-room. It, too, was jammed with well-wishers, filled with laughter, excitement and the deep steady throb of success that pulsed through the Chesterton now. They all knew they had a big hit.

There was one oasis of peace amid the hubbub. From a wicker basket on a table in corner, a pair of sapphire eyes looked out through a latticed door. *Malfi, dear Malfi.* From both lives, he remembered the drill: Cynthia always shut the Duchess of Malfi safely into her cat basket so that she should not get over-excited and run away during the confusion of all the visitors pouring into the dressing-room. Later, when the crowd had thinned out and the party started, Cynthia would release Malfi and carry her in to join the party and partake of nibbles of all the glorious bountiful food.

He met those sapphire eyes; they blinked—winked—at each other and the message flashed between them: *See you later . . .*

34

Under Tottie's supervision, the stage hands had pushed back the scenery and furniture and set up the trestle table at the back of the stage. Front of House staff came round for their share of the festivities. The atmosphere was electric with gaiety; everyone knew they had a hit on their hands, even before the early editions of the morning papers were brought in to confirm it.

'I phoned my review in from Win's dressing-room.' Oliver Crump basked in unaccustomed popularity. 'Well deserved, all of you. I honestly couldn't fault a thing.'

Jilly kept close to Rufus, aware that she was only being tolerated because of her new status under his protection. On the one occasion when she tried to sidle up to Winstanley Fortescue, Miranda suddenly appeared on one side of him, Tottie on the other, and the cat materialized at his feet. Before their combined hostility, Jilly had gasped and backed away, quickly returning to Rufus, who was too busy to pay attention to her; she left shortly afterwards.

A most entertaining soirée. The sort everyone would like to have go on for ever and, for a while, it seemed that it might. But from the trees outside the dawn chorus began hailing the first pale streaks of light in the sky. Yawns were smothered and the first of the party-goers left, rapidly followed by more. There were little items to be taken care of—like getting some sleep before telephones began ringing. with congratulatory calls in the later morning.

Tottie and the stage hands waited to clear away the debris, dismantle the table, replace the set . . . and get some sleep themselves. While they waited, the stage hands slipped outside for a quick cigarette and Tottie returned to the Wardrobe to replenish Monty's dishes for the night.

The cast retired to their dressing-rooms to get ready to leave. The remaining guests melted away. So did everyone else.

A good party, a very good party. The cat suddenly found himself alone on the stage. The table was still set up, lots of platters and bowls still on display. *Wonder if they're all empty?* He had done quite well with friends slipping him titbits, but still . . . might as well see what was left. *Waste not, want not, heh-heh-heh.*

He leaped effortlessly on to the table and lifted his head, letting delicious aromas waft through his sensors. *I do believe there are some prawns left . . . yes, yes, there are . . . there were, heh-heh-heh.*

What's that? A sharp vile odour struck his nostrils. He became aware that he had heard the Stage Door open and close and a strange scuffling sound immediately afterwards. It was coming closer, so was the horrible smell.

Dog! Savage dog! He identified the smell just as he heard the rattle of a choke chain being unclipped and pulled back.

'Your turn to eat, Rambo,' Woody said softly. 'Get the little bastard! *Kill, Rambo, kill!*'

The pit bull tore across the stage, the more terrifying for its very silence. It wasted no breath on barks or growls, all its energies were concentrated on killing.

Monty took charge. The cat leaped from the table to the stage curtain and climbed it in a blur of speed. The dog hurled itself at the foot of the curtain, standing on its hind legs, stretching as high as it could, emitting a frustrated whine.

'Don't you worry, Rambo.' Woody advanced with a nasty leer. 'We'll get him down for you.' He grabbed the curtain and began to shake it.

'EEEEOOOWWW . . .' Monty shrieked. 'YEEEOOOOWWW . . .' He was clinging on—literally —for dear life.

'What's going on here?' a high crisp voice demanded.

Oh Bast! It was Cynthia. And she carried the Duchess of Malfi in her arms.

'*Go back!*' he yowled. '*Go back!*' But it was too late. The dog had already seen them.

'Here, Rambo! Up here! Not them!' Woody's voice rose in panic as he saw what he had done.

The dog whirled and raced for Cynthia and Malfi. One kill was as good as another—and Malfi was the easier target. Cynthia's soft flesh would be no obstruction to him. Not for long.

Cynthia screamed and tried to back away from the charging fury, holding Malfi above her head.

'No, Rambo! No!' Woody raced after the dog. 'Sit! Stay!' He might as well not have shouted. Rambo was out of control.

Cynthia went on screaming. Malfi added her cries.

OH BAST! *Not my darling Malfi! Not my sweet silly Cynthia!* With a blood-curdling war cry, the cat launched himself from the top of the curtain, aiming at Rambo's back, claws outstretched.

Woody snatched for the heavy studded collar.

'What is it?'

'What's happening?'

Drawn by the screams and shouts, the others began appearing in the wings.

Miranda took in the situation in one look and disappeared again.

'Help me!' Cynthia screamed, sidestepping the snapping jaws by a split-second. 'Help me! Mad dog!' Malfi yowled in anguish, knowing what would happen to her if the dog reached her; she struggled to free herself from Cynthia's grasp and run.

Monty landed on Rambo's back—and slipped as the dog veered. His claws scored the dog's side as he slid. The dog turned to snap at him and Cynthia moved a few feet closer to safety.

Woody snatched his hand back just in time; if Rambo's teeth had closed on it, he would have been maimed. Mad with excitement and bloodlust, Rambo knew no master now.

'Here—take these!' Miranda was back, with an armload of umbrellas and walking sticks she had taken from the umbrella stand. 'No! Win! Not you! Come back!'

Winstanley Fortescue, clutching the pole that had once doubled as the Christmas tree, had been following behind her. Now he moved forward, the light of battle in his eyes. He jabbed the pole at the dog, forcing it to retreat.

'Good thinking!' Ace Barron took a walking stick in each hand and went to join Win. Davy and Geoffrey took a

walking stick each. There were only umbrellas left, but
Oliver Crump grabbed one and began flailing it in front of
him.

In unison, they advanced on the dog, driving it back from
Cynthia, so that she had a chance to turn and run while
they held the animal at bay. They heard the door of her
dressing-room slam.

'Who's responsible for this?' Rufus swung an umbrella
as the dog tried to follow his prey into the wings. 'Where
did this animal come from?'

The dog growled and snapped, facing a forest of sticks
and umbrellas. Woody had crossed to the far side of the
stage and taken shelter behind the curtain, trying to give
the impression that he had never been there at all.

'That's your beast—and I know it, Woody Woodson!'
Tottie called out. 'And I've rung nine-nine-nine and told
the police to get here with the dog-handlers—and an
ambulance.'

'By God, Woody,' Rufus fumed, 'I should have fired you
when Win wanted me to. If that thing harms anyone, you'll
never work in another theatre!'

Almost cornered, Rambo snarled and made one more
attempt to escape. With an unerring instinct for the weakest
link in the chain, Rambo hurled himself straight at Oliver
Crump.

'No!' Dame Theodora screamed as the beast lunged.
'Don't you dare hurt my Oliver!' She stepped forward,
heavily-laden beaded handbag swinging and smashed the
metal rim down on Rambo's nose.

'I always knew you cared, Auntie Thea,' Oliver said
gratefully.

At the same moment, three walking sticks flailed at
Rambo, one of them emitting a strange buzz as it landed
on his flank. Oliver pushed a button on the umbrella handle
and the umbrella flew open in the dog's face.

Rambo yelped and, surrounded by hostile forces,
retreated slowly, forced back against the wall, hemmed in.

'Get something to throw over him!' Rufus ordered. 'A rug, a coat—anything! Get over here, Woodson, and control your beast!'

'He's quite friendly, really,' Woody said unconvincingly. 'He's just upset because of everybody having a go at him —and, of course, the cats. Otherwise he'd've been all right.'

Monty hissed sharply from the shelter of the wings.

'Don't tell us that!' Tottie snapped. 'I know you fight him against other dogs. I've had half a mind to report you for weeks. Now you're for it!'

'You're all against me,' Woody whined. 'Everybody from the fat bastard down. A man's got to have a bit of fun.' He attempted to approach Rambo, but the dog bared his teeth and waited. Woody had second thoughts and stayed where he was.

'Keep those sticks moving,' Rufus directed. 'Keep the animal confused and distracted. Don't give it time to think.'

'Cruelty to dumb animals, this is,' Woody protested. 'I'll have the law on you.'

'Go ahead,' Tottie said. In the distance, they could hear the whoop of sirens. 'Now's your chance. The law is going to be very interested in anything you have to say.'

'I didn't do nothing!' Woody spoke too quickly. 'You can't make out that I did.' He began backing away.

'I wonder—' Rufus said. He was not the only one looking at Woody with sudden surmise.

Woody! Of course, Woody. Sullen, dishonest, malevolent—and always around. So much a part of the scenery as to be unnoticed. The cat growled softly. Woody, who nursed a grudge against Winstanley Fortescue because Win had wanted him fired. If he lost his job at the Chesterton, he would not find it easy to get another.

Yes, Woody even fitted the profile: a grudge-holder, an opportunist —and basically stupid. He had taken the chance of hitting out at Win, who was standing on the stepladder with no one paying attention. Perhaps he only meant to cause injury, but he had succeeded beyond his wildest dreams when Win wound up on a life-support machine. It must have seemed a good idea to slip into St Monica's and throw the switch to turn off the electricity and finish the job. Dead, Winstanley Fortescue was no longer a threat; alive, he could—and would—have got rid of Woody as soon as he took over the Chesterton.

Woody, who was too stupid to know, or care, about anyone else who might also be on one of the life-support machines. A murderer, by mistake. He had killed the wrong man. But still determined to get Win, he had returned again to put paint stripper (yes, that was the terrible smell) in Win's orange juice. With security so slack at St Monica's, he would have had no trouble getting in and out, with a bouquet of flowers obscuring his face. No one would have thought twice about seeing someone delivering flowers.

He knew now—and he couldn't talk. Couldn't tell anyone. Oh Bast! Was Woody going to get away with it? The others were only concerned about the way he had introduced the dog backstage. Couldn't they see that anyone who would do that would do anything?

The cat's body shook with fury and frustration; he began creeping forward. There was one thing he *could* do: He could give Woody a few scars to remember him by! Too bad Woody would never know that they came compliments of Winstanley Fortescue!

'YEOW-OW! Get off, you little git!' Woody howled as Monty fastened on his knee, clawing and biting.

There was a thunder of running footsteps down the corridor from the Stage Door and several policemen spilled on to the stage.

The men holding the dog at bay were momentarily distracted, some looking towards Woody, others towards the police. Rambo saw his chance and surged forward, aiming at Monty.

'That's right, Rambo!' Woody yelled. 'Kill it! Kill it! Kill! Kill! Kill them all!'

The cat fought wildly to retract his claws and get away.

Now Woody was trying to hold him instead of throw him off. Rambo zigzagged as the police came at him, but was still intent on his prey.

'Leave Monty alone!' Tottie rushed to defend the cat— with no weapon except her righteous indignation.

'Uuuurrr!' The Instrument agreed. He wielded the pole like a spear, driving the dog away. Then he lifted the pole to bring it down across the dog's back and Rambo ran under it.

'Kill!' Woody demanded. 'Kill!'

Ace Barron slammed both sticks at Rambo. Once again, there was the curious buzzing sound. Rambo yelped and leaped away, racing to the edge of the stage as they closed in on him, then soaring across the footlights into the auditorium.

The police charged after the dog, except for the two who moved to stand one on each side of Woody. 'Inciting to violence,' one of them said.

'Ring down the safety curtain!' Rufus shouted orders. 'Turn up the house lights!' Davy and the stage hands rushed to obey.

The fireproof wall rumbled down slowly, sealing the stage off safely from the auditorium.

In the abrupt silence, Winstanley Fortescue leaned forward and gently detached Monty from Woody's knee. He and the cat clung to each other, looking into each other's eyes with deep sadness and the beginning of resignation.

Ace Barron was examining one of the walking sticks with a puzzled expression. As he touched a knob on the engraved silver handle, it buzzed again.

'I'll be damned,' he said softly. 'It's a cattle prod. No wonder the dog jumped.'

And no wonder Winstanley Fortescue had leaped into space when that had been rammed into the small of his back and detonated. The cat growled and tried to get at Woody again, but Win held fast.

'"Peter Farley, a souvenir of Texas—"' Ace read out the

inscription on the handle. '"From his many friends and admirers. In case of emergency, apply to critics."'

'I don't think that's funny,' Oliver Crump said stiffly.

'Never mind, Oliver.' Dame Theodora patted his hand. 'When you write this up and deliver it to your paper, you won't be a critic any longer. They'll make you a proper show business reporter—and I can hold my head up again.'

Too bad Jilly left early, heh-heh-heh. She'd be hysterical when she discovered she'd missed all the action.

'Win—' Miranda touched her husband's arm—'you're looking exhausted. I think they'll excuse us, if we leave now. You need your rest. You can bring Monty home with us, if you like.'

Not yet. The cat jumped free, staggering slightly as he hit the stage. He was exhausted, too. He wanted to slip away and have a long, long sleep. He couldn't cope with anything more tonight—this morning. It was all too much. He couldn't even think any more, even though there was still much that needed thinking about. He was wiped out, nothing but one instinct left. The instinct that told him to sleep.

What was that? Beneath the rumble of conversation, his ears had picked up the faint scrabbling sounds. Over by the trestle table . . . the remains of the food . . .

He started over, not noticing that The Instrument, head cocked to one side, was following him. Up there, by the cheeseboard . . .

Before he could leap to the tabletop, The Instrument had blundered into it. With a desperate squeal, the mouse raced across the table and launched itself to the ground. Monty pounced.

GOT— There was a cracking of heads, a blinding pain, then blackness . . .

The floor was cold and hard. His head ached abominably. There was too much noise out there somewhere . . . people rushing around and shouting . . .

'Win! Miranda was crying. 'Win—'

'Don't try to move him.' That was Geoffrey. Sound lad, Geoffrey.

'That's right, dear. It might do more harm than good.' Tottie had the right idea, too.

'I'll go get the ambulance paramedics.' That was Rufus, squeamish to the last. 'At least, there isn't any blood.'

'There wasn't before,' Tottie pointed out. 'That doesn't mean— Sorry, dear. No, please, you'd better not touch him. Not yet.'

That was right. He didn't want anyone to touch him. Not even Miranda. He wanted to wait and gather his strength . . . just enough strength to steal away to Wardrobe . . . curl up on a cushion and sleep . . . and sleep . . . and sleep . . .

'What happened?' Geoffrey asked. 'It happened so fast, I didn't see—'

'There was a poor little mouse,' Miranda said. 'Monty tried to catch it and Win—Win tried to stop him. Win tried to protect it.'

A likely story. The Great Lump was trying to catch it himself, trying to steal *his* mouse! It was all coming back to him . . . They had pounced at the same moment—and collided head to head. Again. His head still hurt but . . . Cautiously, he risked opening his eyes.

Miranda and Tottie knelt on one side of him. Miranda's eyes were blurred with tears. Tottie's face was grave with concern. He stared up at them blankly.

There was a faint movement on the other side of him. He turned his head and met two long narrow green eyes that closed, opened, closed and opened again; black ears and white whiskers twitched groggily.

'Hello, Monty,' he said.

It took him a long moment to realize that he was looking at Monty from the outside.

35

SERPENT IN THE HEATHER

100th Performance

HOUSE FULL

'Here's to Win and Miranda—' Rufus raised his champagne glass high. 'One hundred consecutive performances, despite Win's, er, health problem.

'And here's to—' he moved on quickly—'Peter Farley. We're delighted to welcome him back into the cast tonight after his, er—' Another health problem, he moved on even more quickly.

'And here's to the one-thousandth performance—when we'll *really* have a party to celebrate!'

Amid the cheers, Winstanley Fortescue twitched his shoulders restlessly. Rufus did run on so. Why didn't he get to the important news? By the one-thousandth—nay, by the two hundredth—performance, the Chesterton would be Under New Management. Winstanley Fortescue's Management.

Not that there was any secret about it; everyone knew that negotiations had been going on since Fortescue's recovery. *No . . . don't think about that.* Perhaps Rufus was waiting until the final papers had been signed and sealed. That would be the occasion for another gala party.

'Well done, Peter!' He'd said it to Farley earlier, but it couldn't be repeated too often. Farley deserved every bit of praise coming to him.

'Thanks, it's good to be back.' Peter looked around with satisfaction. 'I was lucky my replacement got that offer he couldn't refuse for a new TV series.'

'You're also lucky you've got a hard skull,' Win said.

'Yes.' Peter shrugged. 'When I looked up in the mirror and saw that distorted face behind me and something swinging down on my head—it was too late to escape. He thought I was you. He really hated you, Win. If only Rufus had fired him when you asked him to, none of this would have happened.'

'Rufus wasn't in a position to fire anyone just then.' Winstanley Fortescue spoke bitterly; they were still arguing over the back salaries owed to the staff, but Rufus was damned well going to pay them, he could afford to now that the show was a success.

'What were you doing in my dressing-room, anyway?' He'd been wanting to ask that; Peter had had long interviews with the police, but the rest of them hadn't got much out of him yet. He wouldn't ask why Peter had been sitting at his dressing-table—for luck, obviously. Only it hadn't worked that way.

'I was looking for my walking stick,' Peter said. 'I'd misplaced it—or thought I had—but I knew it was around the theatre somewhere. I wasn't worried about it until I, er, saw that picture of you. The peculiar-shaped bruise on your back, that started me thinking . . . To tell the truth, I was afraid I might be blamed—if anyone found the stick and realized what it was.'

'Woody knew.' The police had told them that much. Cattle prods were used by some owners to separate their animals at the dog fights. Woody had recognized it and appropriated it. After using it on Win, he'd dropped it into the clutter of poles and slats, only to find that it had disappeared when he went looking for it later, not realizing that one of his workmates had replaced it in the umbrella stand, assuming that it belonged there.

Woody had been looking for the walking stick in the dressing-room Peter and Geoffrey shared on the night he . . . Monty . . . he . . .

'Are you all right?' Peter asked anxiously. Win was shaking his head, almost dazedly.

'Yes. Fine. That is . . .' Win looked uncomfortable. 'I seem to have had some strange . . . illusions . . . dreams . . . while I . . . Sometimes they come back to me . . .'

'Funny thing, head injuries.' Peter could sympathize. 'I seem to be all right that way myself. Barring the occasional nightmare.'

What dreams may come . . . Win knew suddenly that Monty was there staring at him. He always knew when the cat was looking at him—and vice-versa, it seemed. Monty had moved back into the Chesterton and refused to leave it. Not that he had tried to lure Monty back to the house. It seemed almost as though they had been so close that they had mutually decided it was time to put a bit of distance between them again. More comfortable for both of them. Not, of course, that he believed for a moment . . . Not now that he was back in full strength and health again . . .

Monty was regarding him intently.

'Yes, yes, of course, old chap.' Winstanley Fortescue quickly piled a plate with choice prawns, slices of roast beef and chicken and set it down in front of the cat.

'Still spoiling Monty, I see,' Tottie said approvingly. She was wearing a new dress—he had insisted that her back wages be paid before he agreed to begin talks with Rufus. She looked splendid and was a lot more relaxed these days.

'Monty deserves it.' Miranda was with her. 'He was practically nursemaiding Win through the bad days.' That was how she thought of them: 'the bad days'. But they were over now. From now on, all the days were going to be good.

'You're looking radiant, my love.' He had meant to tell her before. 'I haven't seen you all afternoon.'

'No,' Miranda said, 'I've been busy.'

'Peter,' Tottie said, 'why don't you and I go and get some more champagne?' She took his arm firmly and led him away.

'Busy doing what?' Winstanley Fortescue recognized the lead-in to a big scene when he saw one.

'I've been to see a friend of Sir Reginald's—' She hesitated.

'And—?' For a moment, cold horror enveloped him. He wasn't, unbeknownst to himself, worsening, was he? The doctors hadn't been giving Miranda bad news? No, no, Miranda didn't look disturbed. In fact, she looked quite happy.

'Win,' Miranda said, 'I'm leaving the show at the end of the month. I've talked to Tottie, she can take over Cynthia's part and Cynthia can step up into mine.'

'But . . . ? Miranda . . . ?'

'Yes, darling,' she said. 'And everything's going to be all right this time. I didn't want to say anything until I was sure. I had a scan this afternoon. We have a perfectly-formed healthy daughter on her way to us.'

'Wonderful! Marvellous! The best news in the world!' He turned to embrace her—and suddenly caught Monty's eye.

Monty looked away guiltily. He caught up a slice of roast beef and, still not looking at Win, backed into a corner and crouched over it, defying the world.

'Win—?' Miranda was waiting for the kiss she had every right to expect. 'Win, what is it?'

'Uuurrrr . . .' Win was doing some rapid mental arithmetic. He glowered at the cat.

'Win? It's all right, isn't it? You *are* pleased?'

'Yes, yes!' He pulled himself together. 'Of course, I am.' He gave a sudden shout of laughter.

'We must call her Kitty,' he said.